Welcome
trilogy **LO**

Meet Annabelle, Gerard and Diana. Annabelle and
Gerard are private investigators, Diana their
hardworking assistant. Each of them is about to
face a rather different assignment—falling in love!

Their mission was marriage!

Books in this series are:

MARCH #3545 UNDERCOVER FIANCÉE

APRIL #3549 UNDERCOVER BACHELOR
Gerard Roch had given up on love since he had lost
his first wife. He never expected to find himself
attracted to an eighteen-year-old temptress. But
was Whitney Lawrence really what she seemed…?

MAY #3553 UNDERCOVER BABY
Diana Rawlins had turned up at the hospital with
amnesia and a baby in her arms! She didn't remember
how either of them happened. Her husband, Cal, was
determined to get to the bottom of the mystery—
especially as that seemed to be the only way he could
save his marriage!

Rebecca Winters, a mother of four, is a graduate of the University of Utah. She has won the National Readers' Choice Award, the *Romantic Times* Reviewer's Choice Award and been named Utah Writer of the Year.

What others have said about Rebecca Winters:

Of **Undercover Husband***
"Once again Rebecca Winters delivers a topnotch reading experience as she expertly adds a little suspense to a wonderful romance…"

—*Romantic Times*

[*Linked to **LOVE UNDERCOVER** trilogy]

Of **Second-Best Wife**
"A rare gem with a stand-out premise, memorable characters, and an emotionally gripping story of forbidden love."

—*Romantic Times*

Of **Three Little Miracles**
"Featuring splendid characters and heart-tugging scenes, Ms. Winters spins a delightful tale in which love conquers all."

—*Romantic Times*

"The first lady of Utah romance novels."

—*Affaire de Coeur*

"Winters weaves a magic spell that is unforgettable."

—*Affaire de Coeur*

Undercover
Fiancée
Rebecca Winters

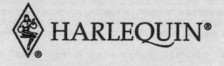

TORONTO • NEW YORK • LONDON
AMSTERDAM • PARIS • SYDNEY • HAMBURG
STOCKHOLM • ATHENS • TOKYO • MILAN • MADRID
PRAGUE • WARSAW • BUDAPEST • AUCKLAND

ISBN 0-373-03545-4

UNDERCOVER FIANCÉE

First North American Publication 1999.

CHAPTER ONE

"ANNABELLE? Don't leave yet. Roman wants to see you."

Annabelle Forrester had been headed for the back door of the LFK Associates International, Roman Lufka's detective agency when she heard Diana call her back.

"Do you know what it's about? I need to get down to the police station." Today was a black day. The busier she stayed, the better.

Diana Rawlins, the receptionist who was one of Annabelle's good friends, was finishing up a telephone call. She shook her head, then covered the mouthpiece and whispered, "All I know is that it sounded important."

Annabelle loved her boss, Roman Lufka. If it were anyone but him asking her to stick around, she would have said she was sorry and left anyway because she didn't want to inflict her pain on other people. But she admired him too much and owed him too much to ignore his request.

Needing something physical to do, she went in the kitchen and brought Diana a fresh cup of coffee. Not only was Roman's receptionist the nicest person Annabelle had ever met, she was a real beauty with golden blond hair to die for.

As a little girl, Annabelle had always wanted to

look like the princesses in the fairy tales her dad read to her.

He had chuckled, patted her head and told her to be thankful for the lovely brown hair with which God had blessed her.

Not satisfied with that answer, she'd asked him what kind of brown. He'd responded that the color reminded him of the smooth horse chestnuts that fell from the tree outside their house.

At that comment she'd run out the door to examine one closely. They looked kind of reddish brown in the sunlight. There was nothing she disliked more than red hair. From that point on she had worn it short.

Now that she was older, she'd come to accept what she considered her crowning flaw, and had allowed a stylist to make the most of it. But she could be forgiven for wishing she'd been endowed like her friend.

"Finally," Diana sighed after hanging up the receiver. "Any news yet on Mr. Vanderhoof's missing Honda?"

"Yes. I found it yesterday morning, but the paperwork hasn't caught up with it yet. Last night the police got a positive ID on the gang member who had stolen it for a drive-by shooting."

"You're kidding! That was fast work. Roman's going to be impressed."

"I hope so. Sometimes things fall into place like that."

"Where did you find the car?"

"At D and G Body and Paint."

"How did you know to go there?"

"I didn't. I just started with A and A Paint, and

worked my way down the list. The boy who stole it knew it was hot. I figured he would go in for a paint job. I was right. He had it done in fire engine red.''

"But how did you know it was the right car?"

"For one thing, red is that gang's favorite color. For another, Mr. Vanderhoof lost the cap to his oil a long time ago. All I had to do was look under the hoods until I found one covered in tinfoil and held in place with an elastic band.''

Diana shook her head. "You're amazing. Have you told Mr. Vanderhoof his car has been found?''

"Yes. He's pretty happy it got stolen. He always did want to buy a red car but never had the courage. When the police told him he could pick it up this morning, I hear he called in for a substitute teacher. No doubt he's out cruising around in it right now. Before the day is over, the police will probably have to bring him in on a speeding charge.''

Diana laughed. "By the way, I have a message from Gerard.''

"Really.''

There was only one man who had ever broken Annabelle's heart and he lived in Phoenix, Arizona, which might as well be on another planet. Since that awful night a year ago when everything had fallen apart, Annabelle hadn't been able to get emotionally involved with another man. But she had to admit Roman's top PI, Eric-Gerard, whom she always called Gerard rather than Eric, had come closest to breaking down a few barriers.

"He says he wants to start over again and wonders if you would have dinner with him tonight.''

"I have other plans this evening."

"That's what he was afraid you would say. I'm supposed to give him your answer when he calls in later because Roman assigned him to work with Chief Gregory on that Utah Steel bombing case this morning and he had to leave here over an hour ago."

"Gerard's not serious about us, Diana. You and I both know he's never gotten over his wife's death."

"The same way you've never stopped thinking about your ex-fiancé?"

Diana was too perceptive for her own good.

"Annie? I'm sorry if I said something wrong."

The constricting band around her chest tightened. "You didn't. I'm just being extra sensitive because it was a year ago today I broke off my engagement to him."

Diana's eyes filled with compassion. She reached out and patted her arm. "I didn't realize."

"It's okay. It *should* be okay. I should have gotten over him a long time ago."

"You mean the way Gerard should have gotten over Simone."

Annabelle nodded.

"Apparently you both fell in love with people who were unforgettable."

"I wish to heaven I'd never met him."

"Annie? If you're this broken up after twelve months' separation, maybe you ought to contact him and find out if he feels the same way."

Annabelle's head flew back. "I know for a fact he's involved with someone else. But even if he weren't,

I would never try to call or see him again. When we said goodbye, it was final.''

Diana's brows lifted. "It doesn't sound final to me.''

"I don't want to talk about it." She didn't want to think about what it felt like to be entwined in his arms, but certain memories continued to flash through her mind without her permission. Memories that sent a wave of suffocating heat through her body.

"Annie?"

Annabelle's face felt hot.

"Roman just buzzed me. You can go in. Since you found the Honda, maybe he's already heard about it and is assigning you a new case.''

"Maybe." *But I'm working on one for Trina Martin right now.* "Thanks, Diana.''

She headed for Roman's inner sanctum. As she approached the doorway, she could hear another male voice talking. Her boss wasn't alone.

"Roman?" She tapped on the door which was ajar. Through the opening she glimpsed the back of a tall, dark-haired man in a conservative blue suit who looked like the number one lineman for the Green Bay Packers.

Her eyelids fluttered closed because there was only one man in the universe who looked like that, who had broad shoulders and powerful thighs like that.

But it couldn't be. He didn't know where she worked, and he had no reason to be in Salt Lake.

"Come on in.''

She opened her eyes again, but she couldn't do Roman's bidding because the other man had turned around, freezing her in place with his brilliant blue gaze which was as familiar to her as her own face.

"Hello, Annabelle," came the deep, vibrant voice she'd loved so well. "It's been a long time."

Dear God. It *was* Rand.

Her eyes darted back to Roman in absolute panic. He knew she'd once been engaged to Rand Dunbarton and how shattered she'd felt after the breakup. So how could her boss, how could Diana, be so cruel as to spring him on her like this without warning? She'd never known either of them to hurt anyone.

The shock was so great, Annabelle felt her body go from burning heat to icy cold. There was a strange buzzing in her ears. She wondered if she was going to faint even though she'd never passed out before in her entire life.

Rand must have seen the blood drain from her face because she heard an unintelligible epithet escape his lips before he was at her side, helping her into the nearest chair. His large hand slid to the back of her neck with the ease of long accustomed habit.

"Put your head down for a moment and keep it there till the dizziness passes."

The voice of command. Rand had no idea how he came across to other people. He took charge without even thinking about it. For once she followed his suggestion because she was too weak and lethargic to do anything else.

With his fingers brushing intimately against her skin, his body so close she could feel his warmth, there was an air of unreality about the whole situation.

It didn't seem possible that Rand was really here,

or that he was touching her in an old familiar way, as if he had every right and was truly concerned.

The last time they'd been together, they'd said unforgivable things to each other and she'd given him back her engagement ring.

Rand had been so forbidding in his anger, she hadn't known he could get like that. It had been a devastating experience, one she'd never been able to erase from her mind. Since then there'd been no contact. Nothing.

Roman handed her a glass of water and told her to drink. "If you're still feeling light-headed, you need to lie down. We can put this meeting off until another time."

What meeting?

She drank thirstily and handed him back the glass. Rand's palm was still molded to her neck.

"I'm all right." She sat straight up so he would break the contact. "I—I went off without breakfast this morning and should have known better."

For an infinitesimal moment her eyes met Rand's. His said he *knew* why she'd almost fainted, but if it made her feel better to pretend otherwise in front of Roman, so be it.

Nothing got past him. He made a formidable adversary. That's why he was the owner of Dunbarton Electronics, one of the top computer companies in the nation. Even more impressive, he'd been the cover man on the March issue of *Today's Fortune,* the computer industry's vaunted magazine.

It had taken Annabelle a week before she'd broken down enough to read the accompanying article. To her consternation she'd devoured every word, every photograph, hungry for any news of him after such a long time. The bio on him made mention of a special woman in his life who was destined to be his wife in the near future, but it didn't give a name. The news couldn't have wounded her more if she'd been stabbed in the heart.

"Annabelle?" Roman interjected. "Since no introduction is necessary, I'll get straight to the point. Rand has come to us for help with a problem that is right up your alley."

She sucked in her breath. "I moved back to Salt Lake from Phoenix a year ago...I can't imagine what any of this has to do with me."

Annabelle had never been rude to her boss. He was the greatest guy on earth, but he couldn't possibly know what this unexpected meeting with Rand was costing her.

She didn't honestly think Roman had engineered it. *Which meant it was Rand's doing. Why?*

When they'd parted company a year ago, enough pain had been inflicted to last a lifetime. She'd had to pick up the pieces and start over again. When she returned home to Salt Lake and Roman took her on as one of his PI's, a certain amount of healing had begun to take place. She'd been making progress.

How dare Rand trespass on her territory after all this time and destroy the world she'd been creating for herself without him!

"The Salt Lake customer service department of my company is in serious trouble."

She folded her arms in the hope of looking more

confident than she felt. "I'm sorry to hear it, but I still don't know what your problems have to do with me."

Rand's jaw hardened perceptibly. For a fleeting moment she derived pleasure because he wasn't as in control as she'd first assumed.

"It appears a hacker has broken in on the lines and is wreaking havoc with the clientele by giving them false information and causing their hard drives to crash."

A *hacker?*

Just last week Trina Martin had called the agency because her eighteen-year-old boyfriend, Bryan Ludlow, a computer genius who didn't get along with his family, had disappeared from his home and had been missing a week. The police assumed it was a kidnapping case and they were looking for him.

Trina believed he'd vanished on purpose. She wanted Annabelle to find him before he did something bad to embarrass his father, millionaire Daniel Ludlow, a prominent businessman who was going to run in Utah's next race for the governor of the state. Bryan's disappearance had made national headlines and now the FBI was involved.

When Annabelle asked what Trina meant about him embarrassing his father, the younger girl said that Bryan bragged a lot about being a hacker. Apparently he'd obtained the password to a major computer company in the Salt Lake area and had already done some things that would make his dad mad with rage if he were ever found out. He sounded too happy about it. That's what worried Trina.

Since Trina's call, Annabelle had run an investigation and she'd turned up some interesting evidence. After listening to Rand, she wondered if there might just be a connection between the two cases.

"The patrons are justifiably angry at what's been going on." Rand's explanation mingled with her own hectic thoughts. "Several dozen people have returned equipment, demanding their money back.

"I've put some of my best people to work on the problem, but so far we don't have any leads. It could be the work of an amateur. But there's the possibility it might be a group of professional saboteurs out to ruin my company and they've picked Salt Lake as their first target.

"I don't know if my enemy is an employee or not. I intend to find out because as of now, I'm going to be personally involved in solving this case. What I need is an expert to work as a partner with me. It has to be someone no employee of mine knows anything about."

Annabelle could see where this conversation was headed, and another pain splintered what was left of her heart. If ever she needed proof that the love he'd once felt for her was dead in the water, his appearance in Roman's office said it all.

They'd broken up because he couldn't handle her career in law enforcement. Being a PI was tantamount to the same thing. Yet here he was at the Lufka agency for the express purpose of availing himself of the very services he'd once asked her to give up for the sake of her safety and their love!

Obviously it hadn't been love that he'd felt for her,

otherwise he couldn't do anything this callous and cold-blooded. Crushed by the revelation, Annabelle rubbed her palms against the charcoal fabric of the slim-fit pants covering her hips.

Dear God, what a fool she'd been. All this time she'd secretly nursed the hope that he still cared. Nothing could be further from the truth!

He'd flown to Salt Lake to find out what was going on in his company. For expedience sake he'd sought her out because she was the nearest person available who knew how to deal with this kind of computer fraud.

After graduating from college with a degree in computer engineering, she'd gone into law enforcement work like her dad. After he died, a friend of his on the force had talked her into moving to Phoenix for a time and working for the police department there.

It would provide a change of scene, give her a little more time to get over her father's death, and she would learn a lot under the leadership of Chief Rivera who was renowned throughout the western states for his success in lowering the crime rate.

Not long after she'd been working there, a bomb threat at the Dunbarton plant in Phoenix had catapulted her into Rand's world and she'd fallen hard. So hard she hadn't seen any problems during their whirlwind courtship and premature engagement until it was too late.

When she'd broken off with him, her life seemed to lose meaning. Heartbroken and bitter, she resigned from the Phoenix police force and returned to Salt

Lake and the little family home she'd rented out during her absence.

In a perpetual abyss, Annabelle couldn't seem to pull herself out of it. Though she joined the Salt Lake police department, her heart wasn't in her work and she simply went through the motions.

That's when her best friend, Janet, suggested she try something different to get a new perspective in life. Why not become a PI, a job which would allow Annabelle to still work in law enforcement, yet allow her more creativity and the freedom to choose her own hours.

At that point in time, Janet was the one voice of reason in Annabelle's shattered world. Taking her friend's advice turned out to be the best thing she'd ever done.

Roman hired her to join his prestigious staff, not only because of her background in police work, but because he needed someone with her level of expertise to handle the electronic fraud cases that came in to the office from time to time. Until now, everything had been going just fine...

Unable to stand it any longer, she jumped out of the chair. "Roman? Could I see you in private? It will only take a moment." The one thing she could count on with Roman—he would always be loyal to his own.

"Will you excuse us a minute, Rand?"

"Certainly."

She didn't trust Rand's pleasant smile. It was about as benign as a quiet summer morning before an earthquake.

As soon as she and Roman had moved out into the hall, he put a steadying hand on her shoulder and forced her to look at him. "He walked in here this morning out of the blue. For the record, I've never met or spoken to him until a half hour ago. No one, not even Diana, knew he was *that* Dunbarton."

Roman was an honorable man. His explanations relieved her more than he would ever know. "Thanks for telling me the truth."

"You're welcome. Now that we have that out of the way, you must realize Rand has a serious problem on his hands. He obviously came to us because he needs the best person to help him crack this case and he knows you work for me."

Roman was a legend with the police force, both locally and nationally. He didn't hire people for his agency who weren't the top in their field. She knew he didn't pay compliments he didn't mean.

His unstinting praise of her was humbling to say the least. But this was Rand they were talking about, the man who had turned her world inside out.

"You're a natural for this assignment, Annabelle. I don't have to point out the reasons why. What he's hoping is that you'll put all personal feelings aside. I realize that's pretty well asking the impossible. I understand if you can't deal with it, but it might be the best therapy in the world if you did."

"What do you mean?"

"You've been hurt by your relationship with him. Perhaps if you faced him head-on, you would exorcise the ghosts haunting you. I speak from personal experience. Because I waited so long to realize what was most important to me, I almost lost Brittany." His voice rasped.

She nodded. Roman's wife had told Annabelle their story in confidence. When they'd first met, Roman had been working as a CIA agent, a dangerous job which prevented him from getting married and putting down roots. The struggle between duty and his growing love for her complicated their relationship and took its toll on both of them. But in the end he gave up his job because he loved her too much to lose her. That was their destiny.

Rand's and Annabelle's case was different. He'd never really loved her. All he'd done was make demands. They had no destiny.

"You know what they say about the truth. It will make you free. Maybe you ought to think about that in terms of your own future. But whatever you decide, I'll stand behind you."

Annabelle closed her eyes for a moment. She *was* thinking. If Rand could treat her like this, then maybe it was time for her to take action and show him the same indifference back. Maybe it was the only way to get over him.

Slowly she expelled a sigh. "All right. I'll take his case." *If my hunch is right and Bryan Ludlow is involved in some way, I'll solve it so fast Rand will be back in Phoenix and out of my life before he knows what hit him.*

Roman's compassionate smile actually hurt. He saw too much. "You're stronger than you know, Annabelle. I'll be behind you all the way."

Having Roman on her side meant everything. "Before I go back in there, I need to discuss something with you first. It's about the disappearance of the Ludlow boy.''

''His parents have already asked me to look into it.''

Annabelle blinked in surprise.

''What do *you* know about it?'' he asked in a wry tone of voice.

In a matter of seconds she related the crux of her meeting with Trina, and the possible link to Rand's problem.

He grinned. ''This is one for the books. Technically speaking, our hands are tied because of FBI involvement. Unofficially however, you can stay her confidante and continue to probe, in case you should find a connection to Rand's crisis which would be a real coup.

''We'll both keep the lines of communication open with Trina and the Ludlows and see where things lead. If you can prove a tie-in, you'll actually be helping two people without getting your hands slapped by the authorities for withholding evidence.''

''That's what I was thinking.''

''Triple kudos for tracking down that Honda. Someone downtown called me on my cellular this morning. Apparently Mr. Vanderhoof has been singing your praises. You've made quite a conquest there. Better be careful. He's a widower, and thinks you're the most adorable creature to come along since Marilyn Monroe.''

Annabelle groaned.

''As I've said before, it's good to have you on the

team. Rand knew where to come to get results, Annabelle. Good luck."

"Thanks. I'm going to need it."

"Any time you want to talk, I'm available."

"I know that."

"Good. So I'll leave you to deal with him." There was a slight pause. "It isn't often that a PI and her client have already made a connection which is so vital in our business. Because the ice has already been broken, so to speak, let it work *for* you, Annabelle."

She nodded. In Rand's case it was more like an iceberg that had been split apart by nature's force. What you saw jutting above the surface of the water was pure camouflage for the huge mass of indecipherables below.

Praying she could carry this off so he would never know what his unexpected entry into her life had done to her, she walked back to Roman's office where Rand lounged indolently in a chair, waiting...

She refused to look him in the eye. "Roman has asked me to take your case and I've agreed. Leave a number with the receptionist where you can be reached. Before the day is out, I'll make contact with you. Goodbye."

On that succinct note she hurried to the back room, pulled her cropped jacket from the rack and slipped it on over the fluid jersey top, both in a claret color. It was a good thing she didn't pause for a bagel from the kitchen on her way out. Even if she had wanted one, three of the PI's had already shown up for work and the food was fast disappearing.

The guys tried to get her to hang around and talk

to them, but she told them she was working on a new case. Her best strategies for cracking one usually came when she went for a long ride on the old BMW. She had inherited the motorcycle from her dad. He'd died of a heart attack four years ago last January.

Annabelle had never known her mother, she had passed away following complications in childbirth. Her dad had chosen not to remarry. It had been the two of them all the way. Many was the time they'd ridden in tandem. She felt close to him whenever she got on it, like they were still a team, like he was whispering ideas to her, watching out for her.

It was Spring now. She always started to feel a little better by then. But come September and the blues attacked. By December she was in a dark funk. She couldn't tolerate the blackness of January.

That's when she went on vacation. She saved up all the time coming to her, then flew to Florida with Janet who was a bankruptcy attorney. The two of them lay out on a beach while they took turns reading books to each other.

This last January had been different. The loss of Rand had made it the bleakest, loneliest period of her life. She hadn't been able to get interested in anything, least of all reading. Being on a trip only reminded her of things she wanted to forget. Even Janet proclaimed it a miserable failure and they'd gone home early.

Now, unbelievably, he was back in her life.

She headed into the towering Wasatch mountains east of Salt Lake. Snow still covered their peaks. Halfway up Parley's canyon she happened to look in her sideview mirrors and saw that a motorcyclist was gaining on her. All in black, he looked big and dangerous.

Lots of cyclists tended to ride in packs, enjoying the camaraderie. But without her dad around, Annabelle preferred to be left alone. She couldn't believe it when he sped up and pulled alongside her on the inside lane, adjusting his speed to match hers.

The Lamb's canyon turnoff was coming up. She looked through her mirrors once more to make sure the light traffic was far enough away, then she headed for the side road.

Ten seconds later she saw that the dark stranger was still following her. Surprised at his aggression, she slowed down to negotiate a turn, then came to a stop and steadied her cycle with her shoe.

Still he rode closer.

When he was a yard away from her, he stopped and lifted his goggles. Only one man she knew had eyes that blue. She had to be hallucinating again. Since when did he ride a motorcycle?

"Rand— None of your stockholders would recognize you in that gear. I told you I would call you later."

His mouth quirked. "I know that, but I felt like a breath of fresh air myself. When I saw you head for the mountains, I couldn't resist joining you. Do you mind?"

He sat back on his bike and folded his arms. While he spoke, his eyes darkened with an intensity that she'd once come to recognize as desire.

Annabelle trembled. "That's rather a moot point since you're already here."

She felt his gaze studying her features. "I've hired myself a crack PI and think the time could be more profitably spent by discussing the case over a late lunch."

Actually, he was right. There was little point in running away from the inevitable. "Do you feel like a hamburger? I was planning to buy one when I reached Park City."

His smile melted her bones. "Anything would taste better than falafel."

"Isn't that vegetarian?"

He nodded. "A woman I used to date was a vegan."

Her body quickened. "Since you used the past tense, I assume she's not the one mentioned in the *Today's Fortune* article."

He eyed her intently. "So you did read it. What did you think of the write-up?"

"The reporter did an excellent job of covering the facts."

"Except for the part about there being a Mrs. Dunbarton in my near future."

"Really." Her heart was pounding so hard she feared he could hear it.

"That's right. As for the vegetarian, her eating habits were not the reason we stopped seeing each other."

"I see."

She didn't see at all. In fact the mention of any other women pierced her to the quick.

"Aren't you going to ask me why?"

"It's not something I need to know to help solve your case."

"But you're dying of curiosity."

"What makes you say that?"

His eyes held a dangerous gleam. "Because you've been sending out vibes so strong, I could feel them through the walls of Roman Lufka's office. Admit you're glad to see me again."

Her mouth had gone too dry to say anything else and he knew it.

"At this juncture I think it's important we start off with a clear understanding of certain fundamentals since we're going to be working closely together from here on out."

Her hands gripped the handlebars tightly. "Your love life is not relevant to our business."

"I disagree. Since we're going to have to come up with a strategy to catch this hacker, I wanted you to know that I'm available on a twenty-four-hour basis. My sources tell me that you're not seriously involved with another man at the moment, either, which means you can devote your full time to my case. As I see it, with both of us unattached, it makes things less complicated all the way around."

Annabelle couldn't take much more of this. "I don't know about you but I'm hungry. If by any chance we get separated on the mountain pass, I'll meet you at Madson's Dairy Freeze at the south end of Park City."

"Have no worry. I'll find you."

Her eyes closed tightly as those words resonated in her heart.

CHAPTER TWO

THEY were the same words he'd said to her at the close of the bomb scare investigation she'd headed on the first day they'd met in Phoenix.

When she'd finished filling out the incident report, she'd told Mr. Dunbarton to call into the police station if he had any more concerns. Someone would know where she was.

As she had started to leave his office he'd said in a deep, rich voice, "Have no worry. I'll find you."

The very next day, as she was getting ready to go off shift, Paco, one of her colleagues said, "Annie? There's someone waiting for you out by the Sarge's desk. I didn't know you had a hot date tonight."

She couldn't imagine what he was talking about. There hadn't been an important man in her life either before or after her move to Phoenix to join the police department. Though some of the officers were attractive, they didn't count because of the department's rule about "no dating among the staff."

Actually she had to take that back. Yesterday, while she was on a bomb scare case, she *had* met one man not in uniform.

He was the kind of male you knew existed, but for an act of nature, you would never meet except in your dreams.

Just the thought of him did strange things to her

heart. She didn't like the feeling and had tried hard
not to think about him. To her chagrin he refused to
go away. It meant she hadn't tried hard enough.

"I don't have a date. I'm going bowling with you
and the guys."

"That's good because I have big plans for us *after*
I allow you to win." Paco was very dashing with his
dark eyes and mustache, and he knew it.

"Forget them, Romeo. Two games and I'll be
ready for a shower and bed."

"My idea exactly."

She grinned. "It's never going to happen. I'll get
my bowling bag and meet you guys in the parking
lot."

"We'll give you five minutes to get rid of whoever."

She made a detour to the lockers, then hurried out
to the front desk with her bag to see who had been
asking for her. As she rounded the corner and caught
sight of the man responsible for last night's lack of
sleep, her legs came to a standstill. She honestly
couldn't make them move because they were shaking
so hard.

Yesterday he'd been wearing an expensive-looking
gray business suit and tie. Tonight he was informally
dressed in a black silk shirt and tan chinos. It didn't
matter what he wore. He had the rugged features and
powerful build of an athlete who played contact
sports, like football or ice hockey.

No one seeing him would dream he was the head
of the nationally reputed Dunbarton Electronics
Corporation. His mind fascinated her. His body ex-

cited her. In more ways than one, he was larger than life.

He started walking toward her. "Is that a bowling ball in there?" His blue eyes danced between lashes as black as his curly hair.

"Yes." The ability to talk had left her.

"Did you have to have it custom made?"

"No." She was losing the battle not to smile.

"I didn't know they came that small. It makes me wonder if I could even get my pinkie in the holes."

"Probably not," she chuckled. He had large hands, just like the rest of him. Because of her diminutive size, her mouth went dry just thinking about the rest of him. "How can I help you, Mr. Dunbarton? Do you have a lead on the person who called in that bomb threat?"

"No. I doubt I'll ever know who it was."

She doubted it, too. "Then I don't understand why you're here."

"I found out you're off duty now, and hoped we could go to a movie together. That is, if you don't have other plans." His gaze wandered to the bag she was clutching.

Annabelle stared up at him in shock. To her mind, the Rand Dunbartons of the world traveled in exclusive circles with exclusive kinds of women who didn't have to work for a living.

As far as going to a film, the mere idea of sitting next to his big, solid frame in the dark had already started to constrict her breathing. A movie theater provided a certain atmosphere of intimacy that would be *dangerous.*

Surely he was joking. He might not be sporting a wedding band, but a man like him would never be without a gorgeous, ultrafeminine creature in tow. At five foot two with short curly hair and wearing a police officer's uniform, Annabelle hardly qualified.

"Actually I've already made plans to go bowling with the guys, but thank you anyway."

"Maybe I could bowl with all of you, then you could accompany me. It's a new film just released called *The Cop*. I'd rather see it with the bona fide article like yourself. That way you can tell me what's wrong with the film, how outrageous and impossible it is."

By now her heart had slammed into her ribs. *He was the one who was outrageous and impossible. I want to go with him more than anything I've ever wanted to do in my whole life.*

"I'm sure the guys won't like me tagging along," he murmured, "but since it's a group date, I can't see a problem with adding one more. Unless you're not at all interested in spending off-duty time with me."

"Annie? Are you coming or not?"

She had no idea how long Paco had been standing there eavesdropping. His scowl was meant to intimidate, but it seemed to have the opposite effect on the man waiting for her answer.

"Ms. Forrester was just making up her mind."

Paco's black eyes flashed impatiently before he looked at Annabelle. "Everyone's outside ready to take off."

I should go with you guys. I know I should.

"Maybe you'd better go without me, Paco."

After a pause, "All right. See you tomorrow." He wheeled away from them and disappeared around the corner of the hallway.

"He has too short a fuse to be a police officer."

"He's one of the best!" she defended, furious with herself for not listening to the little voice inside telling her to end this now, before she got in over her head.

"My car's right out front. We can go to the movie, then I'll bring you straight back here."

Annabelle was tempted. It wasn't as if they hadn't already been introduced. She'd spent all of yesterday afternoon with him looking for a bomb that didn't exist. It had been her job to take down the background information on him as part of the paperwork. Everything she'd learned proved him to be an upstanding citizen and member of the community.

How could it hurt to go to one little movie with him before they went their separate ways for the rest of their lives?

Surely she could handle two hours while she pretended she wasn't affected by everything he said and did, the way he moved and breathed. In the dark she could watch him out of the corner of her eye while he watched the movie. Just anticipating that pleasure made her insides melt.

"I've never had a date with a woman who could protect me before. It will be a novel experience."

So *that's* why he'd asked her out. His life experiences hadn't paired him with a policewoman yet. Curiosity, not attraction, had brought him to the police station.

If it came down to who could protect whom, even

with the moves she'd learned and a weapon in hand, she would place her bets on him any time of the day or night.

"A cop movie sounds like a good way to unwind. I can enjoy the chase without doing any of the work. Let me put my bag away and I'll meet you out front. What kind of a car do you drive?"

She noted a glimmer of satisfaction in his eyes. For no particular reason it made her nervous, which was ridiculous. After all, she wouldn't have liked it if he hadn't been pleased she'd accepted his invitation. *Face it, Annabelle. You're hooked.*

"A dark blue BMW sedan."

What else? "I'll be right out."

It had only taken her a minute to stash her bag before she joined him. Because she was so used to doing everything herself even though she worked with a partner on duty, it felt nice to be treated like a woman for a little while. He opened and closed doors for her, cupped her elbow to usher her into the theater. If only her body would stop reacting to the contact.

No doubt they made an interesting sight. A big, gorgeous man escorting a little woman still dressed in uniform. While they stood in line for their tickets she noticed a lot of females staring at Rand, then more enviously at her. Annabelle would have done the same thing if she hadn't been his date. He was really something to look at.

The film turned out to be a cliffhanger. In fact it was so good she forgot he'd brought her along to help him pick it apart afterward. Oddly enough, he didn't appear to be nearly as involved. To her surprise, during several shoot-out scenes he dropped comments about hoping she didn't expose herself to those kinds of dangers. At one point she heard him say that he couldn't imagine her making police work a lifetime career.

His reaction was typical of most men when they found out what she did for a living. The women on the force had to get used to those kinds of asides to survive in a male dominated profession. She didn't really take Rand's comments seriously. At the time she'd thought he'd been teasing her. That had been her first mistake.

"Do you go off duty at the same time tomorrow night?" Quiet had reigned in the car until he'd pulled up next to her compact car in the station's parking lot.

Her heart thundered out of control. "Yes."

"Good. We'll get a bite to eat and go bowling."

She'd been so terrified of never seeing him again, it took her a minute to realize he wasn't prepared to walk away yet, either.

"Have you ever been bowling?" She hated it when her voice shook like that.

"Not in years. But it doesn't matter. I'd just as soon watch you. In fact, I'd ask you to breakfast, lunch and dinner tomorrow if I thought it were possible. When's your next day off?"

By now her whole body was shaking, not just her voice. "Monday. But I have things I have to do."

"So do I. We'll do them together. I promise not to touch you until you tell me I can. I'm letting you set the pace."

Annabelle knew exactly what he was talking about. She knew that *he* knew how much she wanted to touch him, to be touched by him. Nothing like this had ever happened to her before. It was a revelation. Unfortunately her desire to be with him above all else had blinded her to certain unassailable truths.

He'd been deadly serious when he'd expressed his opinion about the dangers of her work and the hope that she would eventually give it up. Six weeks later, after they'd spent every conceivable moment together, he'd proposed.

When he'd put the diamond ring on her finger, he'd let her know that he expected her to have resigned from the police force by the time they were married. "I want a full-time wife, sweetheart."

Aghast that he'd actually made such a stipulation, she spent the next week explaining what her job meant to her, how happy it made her. Why would she give it up? He had his work and loved it. Couldn't they both do what they wanted and enjoy their marriage, too?

The more she tried to reason with him, the quieter he grew. Their relationship underwent a drastic change. At one point they agreed that dinner was a mistake and he'd driven her home without taking her in his arms.

Devastated by his reaction and desperate to get back what they'd shared, she went over to his condo that night, unannounced, offering a compromise. She would talk to the captain about working part-time.

"No," was all Rand said, his face hardened by lines. "Don't you understand? I don't care if you only worked one hour a week. In that length of time you could be hurt or killed. Police work isn't like anything else. If you loved me," his voice grated, "you wouldn't want to put me through torture every time you left our bed to report to your job."

"If you loved me you'd accept it... I love what I do, Rand."

"More than me?" he almost shouted, his eyes dark slits from the strength of turbulent emotions.

"Can't I love both?"

"Of course. But you don't offer me the same choice," he bit out. "When you leave the house in the morning, there's every chance that by the end of the day, you'll have been shot by some lunatic. Should that happen, and statistics have proven that it will, who's going to be in our bed to comfort me at night after a hard day's work?"

"Don't you have any faith in me at all?" she cried out. "I'm good at what I do."

"You think I don't know that?" His hands had formed fists. "But the percentages work against you no matter how expert you are, no matter how well trained."

Her chest heaved. "Is that your final word on the subject?"

"It is."

"Then this is mine!"

Her pain combined with the adrenaline rushing through her body, caused her to tear the ring from her finger and throw it at him.

White-faced he'd said in a forbidding voice, "If

you walk out that door on me, Annabelle, I won't come after you and beg you to come back."

"Did I ask you to?" she flung at him before she fled his condo in agony.

Within the week she'd thrown out every reminder of Rand. After resigning from her job, she'd made arrangements to move back to Salt Lake.

The only thing she couldn't bring herself to part with was her mother's wedding dress, the one Annabelle had planned to wear when she took her vows with Rand. Just a few days earlier Janet had gone to Annabelle's house in Salt Lake and had sent the dress Express Mail.

With tears streaming down her cheeks, she'd packed it in the wardrobe part of her suitcase to take back home with her. It would remain a memento of her mother's, nothing else.

When Annabelle finally boarded the plane, she felt shattered and broken. Her world had exploded and nothing would ever be the same again.

Rand stayed where he was, preferring to watch the expert way she handled the cycle in spite of her small size. It had been a long time since he'd been able to feast his eyes on her alluring body.

A *pocket Venus*. That's what he'd thought of her the first time he'd met her dressed in a police officer's uniform. Everything was there in exquisite abundance, in all the right places. Just sort of in miniature. Amazing.

In her boots she stood about as high as his heart. Her heavily lashed eyes glowed a greenish-yellow

color like those of a calico cat. She possessed a generous mouth and a cap of curly auburn curls he had
to resist tousling. Her small hands fascinated him.
Hell. Everything about her fascinated him.

She'd been part of the bomb squad which had arrived on the scene after Roman's private secretary had
received a bomb threat. In surprisingly short order
Annabelle had determined the scare to be a hoax.

Adorable beyond belief, he discovered her intelligence and humor to be as intriguing as her looks.
He'd never met a woman like her. She had a mind of
her own and could have cared less about his money.
Her advent into his world changed his life.

An elusive creature, he started out right away to
pursue her in earnest. During the chase scene at the
first movie they'd gone to together, he'd fallen in love
with her and had never recovered.

Much as he might want to catch up with her now
and give her a run for her money on his newly purchased Kawasaki, he decided that would be pushing
it. Better to give her five minutes of lead rope before
he slowly tightened the noose.

There was no doubt in his mind that he was defi-
nitely going to tighten the noose.

Twelve months ago, when she'd thrown the engagement ring in his face and walked out on him, his
pride couldn't take it. He'd told himself he was better
off without a woman who didn't need him or anything
he had to offer.

She could stay married to her career as a policewoman and go to an early grave with nothing to show

for it but a bullet in her back. He'd convinced himself that he didn't care what she did.

For the last year he had immersed himself in work, expanding his company with a speed his board of directors could scarcely handle. Staying hellishly busy staved off the pain. Until he'd left for Salt Lake, Caroline had been there to provide a feminine distraction.

But now he realized she had been a mistake. He should never have gone out with her in the first place. Six months after his breakup with Annabelle, they'd met at a mutual friend's pool party. She'd made it clear she'd like to see more of him. Though he found her attractive and interesting, he told her up front that he didn't believe in love and had no intention of getting serious with any woman.

She immediately assured him that she wasn't looking for commitment, only companionship. She, too, preferred an open-ended relationship. Both of them could go and come as they pleased, date other people at any time, no questions asked.

He'd taken her at a word and they'd started seeing each other casually.

But when he called Caroline from his Phoenix office and told her he was leaving for Salt Lake on business for an indefinite period, she'd treated him to the emotional side of her nature.

In a tearful outburst she admitted she was in love with him. Then she accused him of not loving her the way she loved him or he would have asked her to go to Salt Lake with him.

For some time his subconscious had sensed she was

getting too involved. He should have done something about it sooner, but he'd been too driven by the pain of Annabelle's rejection to act on those instincts.

At that point he confessed that he was in love with someone else and had been for a long time. He was sorry if he'd hurt Caroline. Under the circumstances this separation was for the best. He hoped she would be able to forgive him and get on with her life.

As for Rand, he could no longer deny the truth to himself or anyone else. Annabelle was his heart and soul. If the Fates were kind, he would get her back in his life for good.

On that note he gave his bike more gas, his thoughts flicking to the angry customers out there ready to vent their spleen on the powers that be at Dunbarton's. After arriving in Salt Lake and talking to his manager, Rand had hired a local telephone engineer to hook up a phone line which could be patched through to the main office where he was working alone.

The service people on duty for Dunbarton's had no idea he was in town, let alone what was going on. He could imagine their surprise at such a quiet night, especially when there would be no explanation for it.

So far he'd answered fifteen calls, eleven of them complaints about the wretched way they'd been treated on Dunbarton's software lines within the last week. Naturally he wasn't about to let any of those patrons know they weren't alone in their frustration.

The criminal out there doing his best to ruin Rand's company had already created minor havoc in the Salt Lake region. To Rand's chagrin he wouldn't be able to put out any fires, not until he had answers to several questions. Chief among them was whether the hacker worked independently or was part of a ring intent on infiltrating his company which had service centers from coast to coast.

He supposed the person responsible could have picked Dunbarton's on a whim, but Rand couldn't help wondering if it wasn't a troubled former employee who had been let go from the Salt Lake service center at one time or other and was out for revenge.

That kind of retaliation was common enough. Just tonight the headlines in the Salt Lake *Tribune* had announced Utah Steel's plan to lay off several hundred employees. Two hours later all the TV channels were covering a warehouse fire on Utah Steel's property. So far an estimated million dollars in damage had been done by a pipe bomb.

As far as Rand knew, there had been no sign of trouble at any other Dunbarton plants in the country, but he wasn't ruling out that possibility, and had his top people working on the problem right now.

Much as he hated to admit it, Salt Lake could be the first in a series of problems. That was one of the reasons he was here. To get a handle on what was going on and begin damage control.

But if the truth be known, he'd come for Annabelle. He'd never gotten her out of his system. When word came that the Salt Lake customer service center was having problems, Rand had leaped at the chance to fly here himself.

For the first time in a year he actually exulted over

the trouble in his company because it provided him with a legitimate excuse to see her again.

Through a mutual friend on the Phoenix police force, he found out she'd gone to work in Salt Lake as a PI. While on the plane he came up with the plan to hire her to help solve the crisis. He was desperately in love with her and always would be. No matter how long it took, or what he had to go through, one day she would be his wife.

If she needed a dangerous career to make her happy, then so be it. That issue was no longer important as long as they could be together. Asking her to collaborate on his case would prove that he had changed, that he accepted her desire to work at a high-risk job because it made her happy.

But wanting her back and *getting* her back were two different things. She'd had a year to harden. Softening her up wasn't going to be easy. Today would set the tone for the way things were going to go until she ran willingly into his arms once more.

He had no idea how long it would take, but he recognized that infinite patience would play the key role in obtaining his heart's desire. Rand couldn't afford to make one wrong move. Otherwise he'd lose the only thing that truly mattered to him...

He waited until she was out of sight, then headed toward the main highway. When he reached the turn-off, he opened up. Before long he was passing a lot of semitrucks and the occasional four-wheel drive full of teenagers anxious to get in some late spring skiing.

As his cycle ate up the miles, the cool mountain air cleared his lungs and his head. He experienced a feeling of well-being. Annabelle had the right idea. Nature had a way of putting things into perspective.

Whether she liked it or not, she was part of that perspective.

At the thought, a sly smile broke out on his face and stayed there all the way to the old mining town of Park City which had been turned into a playground for the rich and famous.

The place seemed crowded, even for a weekday. Two blocks up the main street and he spied her BMW parked between two vans in front of the Dairy Freeze.

Rand rode around the corner and found a spot for his cycle. Wedging his helmet under his arm, he strode across the street. The local hamburger stand appeared to be a favorite retreat for teenagers.

After a cursory glance, he found her in the last booth and took the seat opposite her. "I ordered for both of us when I first came in," she announced. "Two bacon deluxes, French fries and a chocolate malt. I hope that's what you wanted."

"I'm glad to see you still remember."

Her head was bowed. "Rand? Shall we talk about your case? The only reason we're together now is to try and figure out who is sabotaging your company and stop them. I know how much your company means to you, because of your dad."

"You're right. We were a very tight team. When he suffered that fatal embolism two years ago, I felt like I'd lost my best friend."

He noticed she wasn't saying anything. *Good.* He had her full attention.

"One of the reasons I wanted you to work with me

on this case is because you understand things no one else does.'' The waitress chose that moment to bring their food. "We connected on a very basic level from the first moment you arrived at the building to find that bomb.''

She took a long sip of the cola she'd ordered, then raised her head. "I think it would better to leave the past alone. By the way, while I was sitting here, I remembered some important business I have to do downtown. Why don't you stay where you are and finish your lunch in peace.

"Since I assume you know my address, let's plan to meet back at my house in an hour. We'll discuss your case there. How does that sound?''

"An hour it is.''

Rand fought to contain his excitement. He'd purposely brought up the past to satisfy a hunch that she still had feelings for him. Judging by her behavior, the past was too painful for her to get into. That was all he needed to know.

As she started to walk away with her hamburger in hand, she paused to say, "When you've finished your meal, have a fun ride down the canyon, but a word of warning. Every trucker in America knows Parley's is a death trap. In case you lose your brakes, there's a road for runaway vehicles about halfway back on your left.''

He practically fell out of the booth. "Thanks for the inside information, sweetheart.''

"Since I read about the expansion of your company in *Today's Fortune*, and found out you're worth another ten million dollars since the last time I saw you,

I realize you're the wealthiest client I've ever worked for. I wouldn't want to lose you now. I need a good bonus so I can take my trip to Florida next January."

So that's where she'd gone.

"By the way. Lunch is on LFK. Enjoy."

I'm going to enjoy it all right. And then I'm going to enjoy something else even more.

In fact her mouth was about all he could think about as he roared out of Park City a half hour later. Catching the culprit responsible for the mayhem on his support lines might take weeks. Anything could happen while he fought to win Annabelle's love all over again.

If his cycle had wings, he'd be flying about now because in a little while he'd be alone with her in the house she'd grown up in.

He'd driven past it yesterday, but he'd never been inside. Before he could take the time to visit Salt Lake with her, their engagement had ended in disaster. But that was history.

Rand realized he'd been given a second chance to make things work between them. As far as he was concerned, that meant being with her day and night, for as long as it took. After a year's deprivation, he found her more beautiful, more desirable than ever.

Being with her made him feel like a much younger man in the throes of first love where anything and everything was possible.

He would never let her go again...

Once back in the city, Annabelle stopped at the police station to finish up some paperwork. With that accomplished she headed home, willing her heart to stop hammering because Rand would be meeting her there shortly. But where he was concerned she discovered she couldn't dictate the state of her emotions.

As she turned onto her street, she could hear the bleeping of her house siren rending the air. Rand must have beaten her home and had started poking around her property.

She grinned, wishing she could have seen the look on his face when he triggered the alarm.

The siren was set to go off if someone stepped on either her front or back porch, or approached any windows. Roman had rigged her home with a dozen different devices so she'd feel safe. It shut off after thirty seconds, just long enough for everyone to look out their windows and see what was going on.

By now the neighbors were used to it, and her friends had learned to call first before dropping in. But it always gave any delivery people, or even the Girl Scouts selling cookies a good scare. That made her feel bad, but since she lived alone, she didn't feel she had a choice but to protect herself.

The best part though was the first time Gerard had sneaked around her house at night unannounced, and it had gone off. After he'd recovered, he'd told her she'd better take out another insurance policy. The chances of a person suing her for giving them a heart attack were much greater than if they had slipped and fallen on the ice on her property.

He had a point, but she'd been putting it off.

As she pulled into her driveway she caught sight of Rand leaning against the brick wall at the back of the house, his arms folded.

When she got off her bike, she had to gaze a long way up to see his face. He'd never fit her image of a computer wizard, the nerdy kind of character in school who was painfully thin and wore glasses.

Rand's big strong body, good looks and black curly hair put him in a class all by himself. He was her idea of male perfection. No other man came close.

CHAPTER THREE

Now that she had arrived, Rand was trying not to laugh, but it was hard. The siren had caught him off guard and he'd let go with a belly laugh. He couldn't remember laughing like that since before he and Annabelle had broken up.

It felt good. Anything to do with Annabelle meant you learned to live with the unexpected. Frankly he was glad she'd had such a device installed. It would scare the delights out of anyone who shouldn't be there.

"Shall we go inside?" The wicked look in her eye made him want to pick her up in his arms and kiss her until she cried for mercy. But of course he couldn't do that.

"After you."

With the flick of the remote she carried on her key chain to deactivate the siren, she marched up the stairs to her back door.

"Follow me."

She motioned for him to walk through the kitchen to the dining room of the tiny, yet cozy home where she'd set up a computer and printer. Finally he was getting a look around her inner sanctum. It was something he'd been wanting to do for a long time.

In touching distance of her now, Rand felt huge,

like he was trespassing in an immaculate dollhouse. Except no dollhouse he knew of ever had a computer in it. Especially not a Dunbarton.

Which gave him an idea for another market entirely, but he had other matters on his mind at the moment. Like the incredible way she moved that perfectly proportioned little body of hers through the tidy maze.

"Would you like coffee? A soda?"

"I won't say no to a cola if you have one."

Rand's smile faded when he sat down in front of her computer and discovered it was a CyberMedia, an inferior product with a multitude of flaws.

"Are you another disgruntled Dunbarton customer?" he muttered when she placed a can of Coke in front of him and found herself a seat on the opposite side of the table. *As far away from him as possible.*

"Don't get your feelings hurt, Rand. My Dunbarton is downstairs in my office. I use the dining room to play around with other brands of computers. A nearby electronics shop gives them to me when they can't figure out how to fix them. That way I keep up to date on the hardware your competition is manufacturing. I never know when I'm going to need the knowledge to solve a problem. But I have to admit I've been ready to shoot this computer for some time now."

"Cyber's a cheap outfit. They buy inferior materials. As soon as one circuit shorts out, the whole business shuts down."

"I figured as much. I keep replacing parts, but something else always fails. However that's neither here nor there. Let's talk about your case. Have you learned anything that can help us?"

Though he was on her territory now, she was all business. Rand should have been prepared for that, but somehow he wasn't. He'd hoped for a tour of the house and a little personal conversation, but there didn't appear to be a thin spot in her armor.

"Only that every victim thus far has said the technician was a male."

"When did your company receive its first complaint?"

He might as well be talking to a policewoman. "A week ago, but I didn't fly in until day before yesterday."

"Why did you wait so long?"

Because I had to free myself from certain business obligations so I could concentrate on you, sweetheart.

"My manager didn't inform me right away because he thought he could handle the problem himself. When it became apparent that it was beyond his control, then he called me. By the time I got my people working on it, a lot of damage had already been done and there are still no leads."

"I might have one," she inserted quietly, "but it could be a long shot."

Rand's lips twitched. "Not that I'm not impressed, but how could you have an inside track already when you only heard about my company's problem this morning?"

Her cat's eyes flashed amber, a sign that his remark had gotten under her skin. "Because I've been working on another case. There's the vague possibility of a tie-in."

At that unexpected revelation, his amusement vanished. The whole idea was for this operation to take enough time for him to break her down so she would trust him again. Then they could build a new relationship, better than before. But if that razor-sharp mind of hers cracked the case too soon, it would jeopardize his plans.

"Let's hear about it."

She reached for the newspaper at the end of the table and handed it to him. "While you read the article about that teenager whose picture is on the front page, I'll get something from downstairs I want you to listen to."

By the time she came back with a tape recorder, he'd scanned the story about Bryan Ludlow, the missing Salt Lake teen. So far Rand couldn't see a connection. In fact he couldn't see past the curvaceous woman who epitomized femininity and made him ache to crush her in his arms. It had been too long...

She sat down once more. "What the newspaper didn't tell you is that Trina Martin, Bryan's girlfriend, came to me because she firmly believes he ran away from home on purpose and she wants me to find him before the police do."

Rand sat there in stunned silence as Annabelle proceeded to enlighten him with one amazing fact after another. "...And Trina says he's so mad at his dad, he'd love to get into serious trouble just to make his parent look awful right before the elections.

"She has this hunch that he's gone to work for a computer company using a phony name and may be out to do real damage. I found out he owns a Dunbarton computer and subscribes to your magazines. Trina says he has dreams of one day becoming the head of a company like yours. But don't let that go to your head, Rand."

He almost choked on his Coke, not knowing whether to laugh or cry. No one could cut him down to size the way she could and still make it sound like a compliment. No one was more earnest or adorable than Annabelle when she was following up a lead. In this case, he had a gut feeling she was really on to something.

That's because she's so damn good at what she does. Hell. She already knew more about what was going on with the Ludlow boy than the police and the FBI combined.

Roman Lufka's private detective agency had the reputation of being one of the top PI firms in the nation. He couldn't help but feel pride that she was part of that renowned group.

A year ago he couldn't have admitted that to himself. A year ago he'd loved her with a selfish, possessive love. In his arrogance, he'd wanted her to accept him completely, but he hadn't been willing to let her be the person she was. Because he was a fool, he'd let her walk out of his life. But things had changed. *He was here to change them.*

"In light of that knowledge, I did a little snooping around your service center before I checked out some of the others in the valley. But no one matching Bryan's description is on the payroll of any of them."

Not only was he awed by the speed with which she worked, he was fascinated by her creativity. "Annabelle— If your client is right, then Bryan is doing what most hackers do and is working on his own."

She nodded. "Because he knows Dunbarton's is the best, I think he would probably target your company to make the biggest splash. After all, your face was on the cover of *Today's Fortune*. It would be a real coup to break your password and invade your sacrosanct space. It would make national headlines. What better revenge against his father."

Rand didn't particularly like the sound of that. She was acting almost excited by the prospect.

"In my spare time I've made up a profile on computer geniuses like you and your ilk. You walk a fine line between the legitimate and the corrupt because you have the most competitive minds in the world. Your egos make you feel so superior, you consider yourselves beyond the laws that govern the rest of the world."

One more thrust of her rapier-sharp tongue, and Rand would quiet her mouth in a way that would help satisfy his craving. But it would do irreparable damage to his well-laid plans. He couldn't risk that.

Their glances met over the rim of the can he put to his lips. Her feline eyes were shot with gold. "I stand reproved,'' he murmured, sounding suitably chastened.

For a brief moment a look of puzzlement broke out on her face. She was speechless. A rare phenomenon. But then the old Rand would never have admitted to faults. *The old Rand didn't have the sense he was born with.*

"Around eleven last night, I started calling in on your twenty-four-hour support line to see what would happen. By three in the morning I'd managed to get through to two technicians. You need more help on the service line, Rand.''

"You're right," he admitted. "I'll have a talk with my manager as soon as I can.''

Again he surprised a look of incredulity coming from her eyes.

"Anyway," she began, sounding the tiniest bit flustered by his meekness, "around four I called in again and got this technician." She turned on the tape recorder. "Listen.''

It only took Rand a few minutes to realize that no company could survive with a technician like that. The man who had just hung up on Annabelle had not only been rude to her, he knew his way around computers and would have wiped out everything on her hard drive with the instructions he'd given her, *if* she hadn't been on to him.

"*Lord,* Annabelle. You've got that hacker on tape. You're incredible.''

He reached across to turn off the recorder, purposely capturing her hand in the process. It trembled beneath his before she pulled it away. Rand didn't mind. He'd felt those tremors charge his whole system.

She might be fighting him every step of the way, but her body had reacted instinctively to his touch. *She was as on fire for him as he was for her.* Like genes, the chemistry between two people didn't lie.

"Don't jump to too many conclusions," she warned, obviously trying to break the tension between them. "That person may not be Bryan. For all we know, it could be an accomplice. For that matter, the two cases could be entirely unrelated and it's someone else completely different."

He shook his head. "I trust your long shot. That young man is not only going to embarrass his family. If he's allowed to continue his sabotage tactics, he'll turn off hundreds of Dunbarton customers before he's through."

"Did you hear a dog barking in the background?"

He nodded. "It could be a pet. Most workplaces don't allow animals. With his kind of money, he has probably rented a house or an apartment to set up shop."

Annabelle agreed with him.

"I'd like a copy of that tape for my head security man."

"I think you'd better hold off on that, Rand."

He shot her a penetrating glance, then lost his concentration as his gaze wandered over her compulsively, drinking in every glorious asset. Her short, glossy curls glinted a rich mahogany color in the light.

She was so desirable, he didn't know if he could keep his hands off of her much longer.

"Rand?" she prodded.

He rubbed the back of his neck frustratedly. She had him so wound up, he wasn't thinking rationally.

"Until we can prove that Bryan Ludlow is the culprit, your head security man is the top suspect on my list."

Annabelle was right. It could be someone high up on the payroll right now, or a CEO of another computer company, or a former disgruntled Dunbarton employee.

One of her finely arched brows quirked sardonically. "Have you considered the possibility that it could be a man or woman from your personal life who hired a hacker to ruin you?"

He stared at her. "You mean like *you* for instance," he mocked.

"It's possible," she answered without blinking. "To be honest, I'm surprised you approached me for help."

Rand weighed his words carefully before he said, "There's a lot you don't know about me, Annabelle. You left Phoenix too soon."

Annabelle averted her eyes, shocked and disturbed that his last remark could hurt so much.

He knew *exactly* why their engagement hadn't lasted, why she'd left his condo without looking back. He'd never wanted an equal partner. He'd just assumed that because she was so madly in love with him, she would be content to lose her identity in him. Forget everything else.

Now he was trying to make her feel as if it were *her* fault things hadn't worked out.

Don't let him do this. Don't let him get to you. Stick to the facts of the case.

"As true as that may be, I *do* know one thing... You have a foolproof security system. It would be pretty well impossible to figure out the password. I imagine that if this is Bryan's doing, then he's not working alone. Someone on the inside gave him the information he needed."

"My feelings exactly," he agreed as if they'd never strayed into explosive territory. "Has Trina heard the tape yet?"

Annabelle looked away. She didn't know Rand like this. Normally he was more volatile. His mild-mannered question threw her.

"No. Not yet."

"Maybe we could meet her somewhere and she could listen to it."

"Actually, Roman wants me to keep a low profile on her case. I'm going to have to confine all contact with her to the phone."

Rand nodded. "It's an excellent recording. She ought to be able to hear it clearly over the line."

"That's what I was thinking."

"Why not call her right now? If that voice doesn't belong to Bryan, then we've got our work cut out for as long as it takes."

For as long as it takes.

Those words struck pure fear in Annabelle's heart. Until the case was solved, Rand wouldn't be going anywhere. He'd made that perfectly clear. Already he seemed at home in her house and didn't appear to be in any hurry to leave.

Worse, he was being so pleasant, she didn't recognize him from the implacable, forbidding stranger who'd once told her she wasn't capable of love because her death wish was all that was important to her.

Unable to bear the excruciating pain, Annabelle had removed the engagement ring he'd recently placed on her finger and put it on the coffee table separating them.

He'd stared at it for the longest time before ordering her out of his condo. "I wish you the joy of your career, but don't expect me at the funeral, sweetheart." His eyes had turned to black slits before he'd closed the door on her. As far as she was concerned, he'd just murdered her soul.

"Annabelle?"

Rand's voice jerked her back from agonizing memories. She felt heat creep into her cheeks. Obviously he wasn't in the same torment or he would never have sought out her services.

Because he was no longer emotionally involved with her, he could afford to be amiable rather than intense. She actually found him enjoyable to work with. *That's what was worrying her.*

From the beginning, their relationship had been so out of control and fiery, she'd never even glimpsed this side of his nature. No doubt it was the side the public saw. Combined with his rare intelligence and dynamism, she could understand why he was a pivotal force in the business world.

If he'd been like this throughout their engagement, they might have been able to reach a compromise, they might...

Oh, dear God. What was she thinking?

"I—I'll call her from the kitchen phone. It's a better connection than my cellular." With trembling hands she picked up the recorder and started for the other room, aware of Rand in close pursuit.

After placing it on the counter, she opened the phone directory. School was almost out for the day. That might be the best place to reach Trina.

She picked up the receiver and punched in the number. After a few seconds she heard, "Roosevelt High School, student speaking."

"Hello. This is Mrs. Smith from the PTA Reflections contest returning Trina Martin's call. She needed information to give the poetry club about next year's theme. Would you please get her out of class and ask her to come to the phone?"

"Sure. Just a minute while I see what room she's in."

"Thank you. I'll wait."

Rand's eyes gleamed. "Mrs. Smith," he murmured wickedly, "care for an apple?" He'd helped himself to one from the refrigerator.

She shook her head negatively and turned her back on him. Since their breakup, she would never have conceived of the day when Rand would be in her kitchen, rooting around in her refrigerator, distracting her until she could barely think.

"Hello? Mrs. Smith?" came the tentative greeting.

"Hi, Trina. It's Ms. Forrester. Don't let on who I am, okay?"

"Oh! Okay."

"I have a tape recording I'm going to play for you. Tell me if you recognize the voice."

"Okay."

Annabelle placed the receiver next to the recorder and turned on the machine. Somehow Rand had changed positions and now his encompassing gaze had trapped hers while she let Trina listen to the conversation. Annabelle's heart pounded outrageously.

Finally she looked away, turned off the recorder and put the phone back to her ear.

"What do you think, Trina?"

"That was Bryan," the girl whispered. "I'd know his voice anywhere."

"You're positive?"

She felt Rand's hand give her shoulder a gentle squeeze. *He shouldn't have done that.* It sent sensation after sensation chasing through her body.

"Yes," the teen answered. "How did you get him to talk to you? Where did that dog come from? He doesn't own one."

Annabelle filed that information away, then twisted around out of Rand's reach. "I'll explain everything the next time I call you. Hang in there. If by any chance you should hear from Bryan, leave a message at the agency and I'll get it.''

"Okay. You're the greatest."

"We'll see," Annabelle mumbled because Rand had made her too flustered to carry on a normal conversation. "Better get back to class before someone becomes suspicious."

"Okay. Talk to you soon."

As soon as Annabelle had hung up the receiver, she headed for the dining room, needing to get out of the kitchen and put space between her and Rand. She grabbed hold of the first chair for support.

"It seems Trina was right. Bryan is purposely trying to get in trouble as a way to hurt his father's political career. It appears he and the person helping him are doing a good job of it.

"Once exposed for their crimes, the media will swarm all over the story, garnering the family negative press. Needless to say, when you prosecute Bryan and his accomplice, public opinion will ensure that his father isn't elected."

Rand stood a few feet away from her, making it difficult for her to breathe.

"Possibly." He cocked his dark, attractive head. "Why do I get the feeling that idea doesn't sit well with you?"

"Because Bryan strikes me as a mixed up teenager who's mad at his parents the same way a lot of kids that age are mad at their parents. Unfortunately, his knowledge of computers and electronics makes him more of a menace than the usual rich kid who abuses alcohol and drugs, or runs away with a girl his family wouldn't approve of.''

"Or he has a criminal mind," Rand conjectured.

Annabelle sighed ruefully. "I suppose that's possible, but Trina doesn't think so. She really cares about him and hopes to stop him before he does something really stupid.''

"I'm afraid he already has." Rand folded his arms, drawing her attention to his incredible male physique. "I've probably lost a couple of dozen customers already. The longer he's out there on the loose, the more difficult it will be for my company to maintain its credibility in the Salt Lake region.''

"You're right. Whether it's a teenage prank which has escalated out of control, or the beginning of a true crime spree, there's no doubt we need to act fast to find him.''

"My sentiments exactly.''

His enviable calm was unnerving. She smoothed an errant curl off her forehead, but it just flipped back again. "After reviewing all the facts, I've decided to go undercover as a Dunbarton technician for the first phase of the investigation.''

At this juncture she expected Rand to give her an argument. The old Rand would have listed several compelling reasons why someone else should take over this part of the case. But he didn't say a word.

"A—a lot of talk circulates when a bunch of employees are closeted together. Once I'm a part of that inner circle, I can infiltrate and try to glean information on the person who gave him the password. It would help if I had a list of all Dunbarton employees who are now working or who have ever been let go or fired by your managers since the Salt Lake store was opened.''

"It's in my briefcase at the hotel. I'll get it for you,'' he interjected smoothly. ''In fact, while you're occupied at the service center, I'll put a tracer on the phone and start calling in on the support line to draw Bryan out.''

"That might be difficult to do from the hotel.''

Something glimmered in the deepest blue recesses of his eyes. "Since you're all set up with the necessary equipment here, why don't I use your house as a basis of operation for the next week or so.''

What? If she hadn't been gripping the chair, she would have fallen down.

"It's a temporary solution that should work to help you keep up your cover, Annabelle. You're going to be working at my office in disguise anyway, so you might as well use my hotel room when you're off duty to keep the pretense alive.

"That way we can both maintain our privacy and no one will have the faintest notion of our whereabouts. When we're not sleeping, we'll stay in close touch on our cellular phones.''

His idea was brilliant. She would give him that.

Just when she was screaming for breathing space, he'd come up with a plan she could live with. Any more physical togetherness and she would lose all perspective.

As for Rand, it only went to prove that he looked

at her as a PI who'd been hired to do a job, nothing more. She should be relieved that the situation was progressing without undo complications. Hopefully they would catch Bryan right away. Then Rand would disappear from her life for good.

She lifted her head. "I think you've come up with a very practical idea."

"Good. I'm glad you agree. Why don't I leave for the hotel right now and gather a few things to bring back here tonight. I'll ask the desk for an extra room key."

She nodded. "That will give me enough time to drive over to the service center and get hired before I come back and pack some essentials."

A half smile broke out on his arresting face. It was a look she hadn't seen for a long time. She couldn't stop her heart from turning over. "I'd love to be a fly on the wall when you go to work on my manager. Howard won't know what hit him."

It was hard to swallow. "Let's hope not." Unable to stand his proximity any longer, she hurried to the kitchen again and found a spare key in her junk drawer.

"Here." She took care to drop it in his hand so their fingers wouldn't touch. He made a fist around it. Anxious to be alone with her thoughts, she opened the door for him. "The key fits this lock."

His head reared back. "Do I dare leave?" he quipped.

Struggling to keep a poker face she said, "I don't know what you mean."

"The hell you don't."

"Goodbye, Rand. See you later."

She shut the door after him and waited for the siren to go off when he reached the bottom step. To her shock, it never sounded.

The beast. He'd outsmarted her by jumping over the railing onto the grass.

She ran to the living room and stood behind the curtain at the front window. Finding a crack, she held up a pair of high-powered binoculars Roman had given her for a birthday present and watched Rand drive away on his motorcycle.

He was *laughing!*

Conversely she felt like sobbing, but she didn't have the luxury. It would take her a few minutes to get into her disguise before she left for the Dunbarton service center. Assuming *Howard* didn't go home before four-thirty, she would have an hour to fill out a job application and manipulate him to hire her on the spot.

Forty-five minutes later Annabelle reached the parking lot outside Dunbarton's and immediately proceeded to phone Gerard on her cellular.

He sounded pleased to hear from her, but she told him this had nothing to do with going out to dinner. Instead, she explained what was going on with her case and informed him she needed his help. After he agreed to cooperate, she didn't prolong the goodbyes. As soon as she turned off the phone, she hurried inside the building.

The interview with Howard went even better than

she'd anticipated. After dropping him a juicy piece of industry gossip, she passed the technician's test with zero errors. Gerard pulled through like she knew he would because he was a wonderful man.

After the glowing report he gave Howard about her past work record, Howard fell all over himself welcoming her to the team. He not only showed her where she'd be working, he told her she could report that night and work the ten to six shift if she wanted to.

Annabelle informed him she needed the money and would be there on the dot.

When she pulled her Jeep in the driveway, she was feeling so pleased with herself she forgot to press the remote. The alarm went off as she started up the stairs, bringing Rand to the door.

He was back already? There'd been no sign of his motorcycle. His white smile did amazing things to her insides. So did the delicious odor of steak and pan-fried potatoes with onions wafting past her nostrils. She'd hadn't smelled anything as good in a long time.

"I'm going to assume that you were so happy to see me, you didn't realize that I would reset your gizmo. Sorry if it startled you."

He wasn't sorry at all, but she purposely let that comment pass as she swept into the kitchen and promptly removed her ash-blond wig and glasses.

"I have to admit I'm glad you've been here slaving over my hot stove, but the good news is, I start work tonight. It may be that by morning, I'll have learned something that will lead us to Bryan's accomplice. How did you get here?''

"In a rental car. It's parked across the street."

She hadn't even thought to look. "Look, Rand—I'm quite aware that you are taking precious time away from your work at headquarters in Phoenix. Because of that, I've made a vow to get this case solved in record time. Now if you'll excuse me, I'll change my clothes. When I come back, I'll set the table."

"It's already set."

She wished he wouldn't stare at her mouth like that when he talked to her. Avoiding his gaze, she plunged her hand in the deep pocket of her navy blazer and pulled a mini tape recorder from her pocket. "Here." She placed it on the counter. "I recorded everything Howard and I said to each other. This ought to amuse you while I'm changing."

CHAPTER FOUR

RAND followed her retreating back with his eyes. She looked extremely beautiful, but so different in the no-nononsense business suit that camouflaged her curves, he wouldn't have recognized her except for her auburn hair. With that blond wig and steel-rimmed glasses, her disguise had him completely fooled.

Burning with curiosity over her interview with Howard, he turned on the recorder. Howard's voice blared.

"Thanks for coming, Mrs. Black, but we're not hiring technicians at the moment."

"Your secretary told me, but I still wanted you to see *this*."

"What is it?"

"A couple of samples of memory chips. This one is the new memory chip made by CyberMedia where I just turned in my resignation. They've been installing these in their computers for the last couple of months to lower the base price of their new P.C.'s so they can wipe out all the competition, mainly from Dunbarton's.

"Now—if you'll look closely at this other memory chip, you'll see this is a Dunbarton chip. Check them both out and tell me what you see."

"I don't know. They look the same to me."

Rand frowned. Howard sounded like an idiot.

"That's because Cyber's chips are made with inferior wire which is coated to look like copper, but breaks down easily. Dunbarton uses real copper which is more expensive to begin with, but almost never breaks down. I wrote a paper on the advisability of using copper wiring over other metals in the chips before I graduated in computer engineering."

"*You're* a computer engineer?"

"I put it on my application but I realize you haven't had a reason to read it yet. One day I'll open my own company. Right now I'm getting experience in the workplace where I can conduct my own personal research and put my theories into practice. Go ahead, scrape both of them with a coin. See what happens."

Rand heard a scratching noise.

"You're right, Mrs. Black. The coating sluffs off on this one!"

Howard sounded like he'd just invented the wheel. At this point Rand was as spellbound as his manager by Annabelle's persuasive arguments.

"A Dunbarton computer may cost two hundred dollars more, but the maintenance problems are minor compared to the astronomical nightmares on a Cyber. They can't keep enough technicians on hand to answer all the complaints.

"If you quote me on this I'll deny it. But—their trainers are disgruntled technicians they picked up when Info-Tech folded. Mark my words, within six months Cyber will be losing money and laying off employees.

"By the way, I've got half a dozen other faulty parts I'd love to show you sometime, not only from

Cyber but Space Tel, Tronimania, and Electronic Gadgets, Etc. So far, all my research points to Dunbarton being the one company with the least amount of problems.

"Of course I couldn't in good conscience tell Cyber's customers to sell their computers and go purchase a Dunbarton, but I have urged them to buy Dunbarton components.

"You can keep both chips if you like and send them to Mr. Dunbarton himself in Phoenix. It ought to make his day that his company has wiped out another competitor. Thanks for listening. I'll let myself out."

"Wait just a minute, Mrs. Black. I'd like to talk further with you, but first I want to take another look at your application. *Eileen?*"

Rand listened to a little more of their exchange. He laughed until his sides hurt. Finally he shut off the tape recorder.

"Shame on you, *Mr.* Dunbarton, for finding CyberMedia's demise so amusing," a familiar female voice reverberated in the minuscule kitchen.

She'd come in through the dining room dressed in a pair of gray sweatpants and top. He rested his hip against the counter, content to take in her womanly attributes, especially her hair. The curls looked tousled, like she hadn't stopped to brush them. She looked good. *Too good.*

"I was laughing because you had my manager nailed to the wall in a matter of seconds. I'll say it again. I stand in awe of your many talents, hidden and otherwise."

Like a shooting star, that mysterious smile of hers he loved made an unexpected appearance.

"Coming from you that's a real compliment."

"From me?"

"Don't be modest, Rand. While your talents have put you at the head of a megacorporation, the rest of us are mere peons by comparison."

"Don't forget my megacorporation would be on the verge of toppling if it weren't for you. Any time you want to change careers, you have a permanent position as head of Dunbarton Security." *On top of my personal plans for you, of course.*

Her expression sobered. "I'm afraid I don't do well when I'm tied down to one spot day in and day out."

Whether you like it or not, life as you know it is about to change in the near future, sweetheart.

"How do you think you'll last eight hours on the job tonight?"

"That's different. I'm on a quest."

He smiled. "The list you wanted is on the buffet."

"Good. Just to be safe I'll wear my recorder on the employee breaks as well as while I'm answering calls. If a name is mentioned I can't remember, we'll play back the tape after I'm off duty and check it against names on the list."

He nodded his assent. "Shall we eat?"

"Yes. I'm starving. Everything looks and smells delicious." For the next few minutes Annabelle relished her meal in silence. When she noticed that he hadn't been talking she said, "I had no idea you could cook."

"In high school, while mother was so ill with cancer, I prepared all the meals for the family."

Her fork paused midway between her mouth and her plate. "You never told me that before."

"Probably because I knew if I ever took you to my condo, we'd end up making love. When I found out you were saving yourself for your husband, I decided to behave honorably because I didn't want to make any mistakes with you."

He heard the fork drop.

"After the dozens of hotel rooms I've had to put up with for the last year, you could have no idea how good it feels to be in a real home for a change."

"I'm surprised with your size that you don't have claustrophobia by now."

"I'm managing just fine," he drawled. When her defenses went up, then he knew he was making progress in breaking her down. "Since you've got to get into your disguise again and report for work pretty soon, maybe now would be a good time to discuss the sleeping arrangements."

On cue she pushed her chair back and stood up. He got to his feet, as well. Clearing some of the dishes, he followed her into the kitchen.

"My office is downstairs. There's a comfortable Hide-A-Bed. It might be the best place for you to sleep because it's next to the equipment. There's bedding in the linen closet. I'll get it."

"Let me," he urged. "After I finish the dishes, I'll make up the bed. You go do what you need to do. Oh, before I forget. Your friend, Janet, left you a message on your voice mail. It sounded urgent."

The news seemed to jar her. "I'd better phone her before I leave for work."

Rand pulled a key out of his pocket and laid it on the counter near her hand. "In case I forgot to tell you, I'm staying at the Temple View Hotel, room twenty-five."

When the knock came, Annabelle groaned and pulled the pillow over her head. It couldn't be Rand. He would have phoned first.

She'd purposely placed the Do Not Disturb sign outside his hotel room door so the maids would leave her alone. Since coming off the night shift at Dunbarton's, she'd only been asleep three hours and needed at least three more to wake up halfway human.

To add insult to injury, she'd learned nothing new to help with the case. Last night's phone calls were the usual hodgepodge of anxiety-ridden users who had wandered down strange roads and needed someone to show them the way back again.

The only interesting phone conversation had been the one she'd made to Rand. She'd experienced an unexpected thrill when she'd heard him answer the phone from her own home and knew he would be there all the time.

Only until this case is closed, Annabelle.

After telling him there was nothing to report on her end, she could have talked to him all night. Of course that would have defeated the purpose of her being there. The hardest thing she'd ever had to do was tell him she had to hang up and get back to work.

Maybe Bryan Ludlow had taken the night off because not one person had called in on her line with complaints about the horrible service they'd been getting. None of the other technicians seemed to be dealing with angry patrons, either. It was a quiet night all the way around.

Annabelle had tried to engage at least one of the employees in a meaningful tête-à-tête. But most of them were men who didn't turn out to be the least bit talkative. The women were a little more friendly. Occasionally she would wander by their cubicles for a chat. But on the whole, it wasn't a social scene.

Maybe everyone was too tired to interact on the breaks, or they resented her getting too friendly on her first night at work.

Whatever, Annabelle had come back to the hotel thinking maybe this had been a bad idea. Maybe Bryan Ludlow had grown bored of his own destructive behavior and had moved on to something else.

The knocking on the door persisted, jarring Annabelle from her unproductive thoughts. Then she heard the sound of several female voices.

Annabelle frowned and sat up. Rand had signed up for this room for an indefinite period. The hotel housekeeping staff wouldn't be expecting him to vacate it at the usual checkout time. Maybe someone's child, left unattended, had taken the signs off the doors making it impossible for the maids to know which rooms to make up and which ones to leave alone.

She wished everyone would go away. Pulling the blanket over her head, she was just about ready to lie down again when the door opened and the light went on.

"Rand? Darling?"

The sound of another woman calling out to Rand in soft, sultry tones caused Annabelle to let go of the blanket.

A beautiful woman looking the epitome of every golden-haired princess out of every Grimm's fairy tale, except for her modern day clothes, stood there staring at Annabelle.

Rand's words came back to mock her. *There's no Mrs. Dunbarton in my future.*

She didn't know which of them was the most surprised. The woman's china blue eyes made a thorough assessment of Annabelle dressed in an oversize white T-shirt—her normal nightwear—before her incredulous gaze swept around the hotel room.

Annabelle looked where the other woman was looking and experienced a hot flash as the blood stormed her cheeks.

She'd been so tired when she'd come in the darkened room at six-thirty this morning, she hadn't noticed that Rand's suitcase had been left open on the other bed. There were a couple of white T-shirts that looked like the one she was wearing, plus some polo shirts which were lying on top of the covers. A belt and jeans had been thrown over a chair. He'd also left a pair of socks and some running shoes on the floor.

Worse, Annabelle had put her steel-rimmed glasses and blond wig on the dresser next to Rand's expensive leather briefcase standing near the television console.

The rest of her suit lay on one of those luggage racks at the end of the bed supplied by the hotel.

The sight of Coke cans and a potato chip bag gave the room a well lived in look, as if they'd had quite a night of it. Annabelle had no idea Rand was so messy. Because of her moral upbringing, they'd never lived together or slept together.

"Where's Rand?" the blond vision demanded in a wicked stepmother-type voice. Annabelle couldn't blame her. If the other woman was on a "darling" basis with Rand, then she had every right to know what was going on.

If the shoe had been on the other foot, and Annabelle had walked in on Rand only to find another woman in his bed, Annabelle probably would have had a heart attack from the pain and someone would have been forced to call 911.

"He's at work."

"I see. And who are you?"

"I'm Merilee. Listen, I'm afraid this isn't what it looks like, Ms..."

"Graham." The woman's lovely face had paled. "It never is, *Merilee.*"

Was she the vegan, or the woman mentioned in the magazine article? "I really can explain."

"Go ahead." She stood there ramrod-stiff in her heavenly peach-colored suit and pearls, waiting for a plausible explanation when she'd already suspected the very worst.

Annabelle had to think. Electronic sabotage could be carried out on a local scale by an amateur like Bryan Ludlow, or it could be the work of professionals with an eye to ruining Rand's company from coast to coast and they had somehow inveigled Bryan to work for them.

Because of that fact, Annabelle had to treat everyone as a suspect, even Ms. Graham. To make matters worse, Rand hadn't discussed his personal life with Annabelle, so she didn't know if the other woman knew *why* Rand had left Phoenix to come to Salt Lake.

However one thing seemed fairly evident. Rand hadn't been expecting this woman to visit, be she his girlfriend, fiancée or lover. Otherwise he would never have suggested that Annabelle use his hotel room while they were trying to track down Bryan and his accomplice.

"I'm an acquaintance of his, Ms. Graham. After work I realized that I had gotten locked out of my house, so I phoned Mr. Dunbarton for help. He was already up this morning and getting ready for work when I called. So he told me I could come over and use his hotel room until I could get hold of a locksmith to take care of the problem."

Her eyes had turned arctic navy. "Rand hasn't been to Salt Lake in ages. How do you know him? What kind of work do you?"

"I—I'm a hair stylist," she dissembled. "I specialize in wigs," she added when she saw Ms. Graham had been staring at it. "I've cut his hair before. Yesterday Mr. Dunbarton came into the shop where I worked and asked if I'd give him a trim. He happened to mention that he was staying at the

Temple View Hotel while he was in town on business.''

"So of course you called him the second you got off work and trotted right over here.''

"No—it didn't happen like that. As I told you, I went home, but I couldn't get in. So I drove to a pay phone and called his hotel, hoping he would contact a locksmith for me.''

"And you couldn't possibly have called one yourself.''

"Yes. I could have, but I only had a quarter, and I was afraid that if I lost it, I would be out of luck. Since he said he was always up at five-thirty in the morning, I wasn't afraid to wake him.''

"How sweet. When did you call him?''

"At six-thirty.'' *You're in for so many lies now, you're never going to keep things straight.*

"You got off work at six-thirty this morning?''

"Yes. Our shop is open twenty-four hours a day except Sundays. Anyway, he said I could come over here and make myself at home because he was leaving for work. We never even saw each other. He left a key for me at the desk. It's right there.'' *At least that was the truth.*

"Has a locksmith been called?''

"Yes. He's meeting me at my house at noon.''

"Well—now that I'm here, I think you'd better go before Rand discovers how you've taken advantage of his generosity. I'll give the key back to him.''

The woman hadn't believed a word of Annabelle's story. Annabelle herself had to admit it was the worst she'd ever told, but better Ms. Graham suspect Rand

of being unfaithful than for Annabelle to give away
something she shouldn't.

She was confident that when this case was solved
and Ms. Graham had been cleared of any duplicity,
Rand would use his potent male charm to explain
things to this woman's complete satisfaction. No
doubt at some future point Ms. Graham was in line
to become *Mrs.* Rand Dunbarton.

A devastated Annabelle held back the tears that
would gush later, when she was in the privacy of her
own home. *Alone.*

Under the circumstances it was probably a good
thing Ms. Graham had entered Rand's hotel room uninvited. The woman's unexpected appearance had
given Annabelle the wake-up call of her life!

"I'll get dressed right away."

"You do that. I'll give you exactly five minutes to
be gone from here."

To her horror, the other woman stayed planted
where she was. Annabelle leaped from the bed and
disappeared into the bathroom to get dressed. There
wasn't a moment to lose. She needed to get Rand on
the cellular phone, but it was still under the pillow of
the bed where she'd been sleeping.

When she emerged a few minutes later, she found
Ms. Graham on the hotel phone, demanding that
someone get Rand on the line. Obviously she'd called
the Salt Lake store and wasn't about to be put off.
That gesture led Annabelle to question whether Ms.
Graham knew anything at all about the problems be-
setting Rand's business.

But in any event, the present situation couldn't be

allowed to continue. Annabelle found some hotel stationery and jotted down her home phone number. Then she walked over to the other woman who appeared to have been put on hold.

"Mr. Dunbarton said he would leave this number in case I ran into any problems," Annabelle murmured. "I imagine it's a private line to his office. You shouldn't have any trouble reaching him."

"Just one minute!" she cried out furiously. "Since you seem to know so much about every intimate detail of his private life, you're not going anywhere until I've had a talk with him."

Her glorious golden hair flew as she snatched the paper from Annabelle's fingers and jabbed the phone buttons to make the call. In that split second, Annabelle reached for the cellular phone beneath the pillow and slid it inside the pocket of her blazer.

"Don't you dare leave this room," she hissed when Annabelle started for the door with her wig and glasses in hand. "I've taken all I'm going to take. Now I want to hear Rand's version and you're going to stay to hear it."

"I'd rather not. I'm only a friend."

"Like hell you are."

Annabelle felt worse than a worm as she was forced to listen to Ms. Graham's blow-by-blow version of what had happened since she'd arrived in Salt Lake, especially the part about talking the hotel maid into letting her into Rand's room.

Between bouts of rage and sobs, her words were practically incoherent. Annabelle had the grace to feel sorry for her. She was obviously very much in love with Rand. Annabelle could relate completely. She felt like sobbing herself. *Howling.*

In time the other woman grew quiet. Undoubtedly Rand had begun his explanation. Whatever he said seemed to be working. Not a sound escaped Ms. Graham's lips. Eventually she hung up the receiver and turned to Annabelle. Her cheeks were highly flushed and her blue eyes held a strange glitter.

"When I met Rand, he said he wasn't involved with anyone," she began in a low, trembling voice. "It's so strange." She shook her head, acting almost as if she were talking to herself. "You think you know a man. You think you know what he wants, when all along he's wanted something else. *Someone* else."

Annabelle felt distinctly uncomfortable. This woman was bearing her soul to a perfect stranger.

"You can drop the act and stop acting so coy. It's obvious he wants *you.* Apparently it's been you for a long time."

It was Annabelle's turn to tremble. Rand had allowed this woman to go on believing a lie, which meant Ms. Graham could still be a suspect in his eyes. But didn't he have any idea how much damage he had done to their relationship by sustaining it?

This woman adored him, had come all the way from Phoenix to be with him. Annabelle hadn't thought he could be so cruel.

"You're wrong, Ms. Graham." She spoke forcefully. "I told you before. We're only passing acquaintances."

"Well—maybe for you it's only a passing thing,

but he's painfully in love with you. That much I *do* know."

Annabelle's hands spread apart in frustration. "You're just saying that because you're so upset. I know how awful I would have felt if the same thing had happened to me."

"Stop trying to cover everything up," she countered quietly. "I happen to know Rand wasn't lying just now."

All Annabelle could think about as Ms. Graham left the room and shut the door was that Rand had gone into the wrong business. He played his role so convincingly, he ought to have been an agent for the CIA. In fact, that was the first thing she told him when she got him on the phone seconds later.

After she'd given him a strong piece of her mind he said, "If you've finished, I suggest you crawl back in bed and go to sleep. I figured you wouldn't be up until three or four this afternoon at least.

"By the time you arrive for dinner, the chicken I've been marinating since last night will be ready. I hope you love shish kebabs as much as I do."

"Of course I love them, but that's not the point, Rand. She's hurting."

"So's my company," he came back on a much more serious note.

"But—"

"I didn't invite her here, Annabelle, but some people don't wait for an invitation."

"If they're in love, they shouldn't have to!" she blurted.

"That's assuming, of course, that both parties are of the exact same mind."

"You mean you're not?"

"No, I'm not, and Caroline knew this a long time ago. She just didn't believe it until today."

Annabelle had this suffocating feeling in her chest because he sounded so sincere.

"Unfortunately she thinks *I'm* the reason, Rand. It was horrible when she caught me asleep in your bed. If you had seen the look on her face... By just being here I hurt her horribly."

"Your compassion does you great credit, Annabelle."

"Don't you dare laugh, Rand Dunbarton."

"I'm not laughing."

"You always laugh about everything," she grumbled.

"How do you know?"

"Because I've watched you through the binoculars when you didn't think I was looking," she confessed before she realized what she'd just said.

There was a quiet pause. "Well, if you had them trained on me now, you would discover I'm in a very different frame of mind."

That makes two of us. "I don't think I'm going to be able to go back to sleep."

"If that's the case, why not come home and I'll have a nice cold drink waiting for you. We'll talk about the case."

She bit her lip. "It's not going very well."

"It's only day one. These things take time. We'll talk about it and review our strategy. I've got that list of names we can review. If nothing happens after a few days, we'll put Plan B into action.''

"Plan B?"

"The one you already have in mind. I can't wait to hear it. That marvelous brain of yours never sleeps.''

"Unfortunately my *marvelous* brain isn't worth two cents at the moment."

"That's because you're tired. You'll sleep better in your own bed.''

"Not during the day."

"That's right. The alarm. You never know when some poor unsuspecting fool will approach your door and set it off. If you want, I'll deactivate it while you catch up on your rest. Naturally I'll stand guard.''

That was the best idea she'd heard yet. "You wouldn't mind?''

"As I told you earlier, hotel rooms are lonely places. I avoid them as much as possible."

Looking around Rand's hotel room, she could only agree with him. "I'll be home in ten minutes."

CHAPTER FIVE

"I'M SORRY I slept so long. It's almost time for me to go to work!"

Annabelle's eyes were hooded and she moved rather tentatively, as if she might stumble given the slightest nudge. One cheek seemed more flushed than the other. Rand loved the way she looked when she first got up. Warm, disheveled and desirable. It was all he could do to keep his hands in his pockets.

Things couldn't be working out better. Though he would never have hurt Caroline intentionally, the scene at the hotel this morning had sent the definitive message; whatever the two of them had shared in the past, it was finally over.

As for Annabelle, she would never be rid of him, but he realized he had to proceed carefully. One false move at this point…

"The food's in the oven. Come in the dining room and we'll eat."

"I feel like a fraud," she said a couple minutes later, having devoured one skewer of vegetables and chicken. "You're paying me to help solve a huge problem for your company and now you're waiting on me hand and foot when I haven't done anything to earn my keep yet."

"Wrong. You've let me play house with your

82

things. There's nothing I enjoy more. My greatest fear is that you'll never get it all put back together again.''

"Well, if your hotel room is any indication—''

The smile he flashed made her breath catch. "You noticed.''

"Umm... One of your many sins I'm still learning about, no doubt.''

"When you've got time, I'll confess a few more. Here, have another shish kebab.''

"This is the best food I've ever tasted. Here I was thinking you would make a great CIA agent when it's obvious you've missed your calling as a gourmet chef at some divine spot on the Mediterranean.''

Rand poured them the wine he'd purchased. "You mean like France or Italy.''

"Or Minorca.''

"One of the islands off the coast of Spain. Minorca it is.''

She darted him a quizzical look. "What do you mean?''

"My bonus to you.''

"I was only kidding about that,'' she murmured, averting her eyes.

"*What?* The bonus, or Minorca?''

"Both.''

"I *wasn't.*' He drank his wine in one go. "What were you saying about the CIA?''

She shook her head. "Nothing. I think I'd better get dressed. Thank you for the delicious dinner, a-and the wine.''

The slight stammer proved another endearing trait. "You're welcome.'' He followed her as far as the living room. "I've been looking over the names of the employees who were let go. There aren't very many. From the comments, most were unreliable or had too many sick days. There's nothing in their histories to suggest suspicious or unlawful behavior."

He heard her deep sigh. "Which puts us back at square one. We're just going to have to hope that one of these nights Bryan Ludlow breaks down and starts causing trouble again so we can catch him in the act."

"I'll be working on it from my end and we'll keep in touch throughout the night."

She nodded. "When do you sleep?"

"I manage. By the way, your mail came. I put it on your desk downstairs. You also received two faxes. I left the printouts there, too."

"What did they say?"

"I have no idea, but both were from your bankruptcy friend. Do you want me to bring them upstairs for you while you're getting ready?"

"No. I'll look at them later. Thank you anyway."

"Annabelle?"

"Yes?" She sounded breathless.

"Do you have any idea how much I want to kiss you?"

She backed away from him. "That's because you had a fight with Ms. Graham."

"Caroline and I did not have a fight. We said goodbye forever."

"Then all the more reason why you're needing comfort."

"Your psychoanalysis is wasted on me. I've kissed

you before and know what I'm missing. Let's at least be honest about that.''

"I admit the physical side of our relationship was pretty overwhelming. It blinded us to the realities. That happens once in a while to the most unlikely couples. Luckily we found out soon enough to save ourselves a lifetime of grief. Now I've really got to hurry or I'll be late for work.''

Rand was getting used to her salvos. The more she fought him, the more he knew his plan was working. "Don't worry about it. I own Dunbarton Electronics.''

"Exactly.'' Her voice shook. "Since you hired me to do a job, I'd like to impress you with my performance. Thanks again for dinner.''

As soon as she withdrew, Rand did the dishes and went downstairs. He decided to hide out before she found an opportunity to tell him their arrangement wasn't working. If she asked him to leave, then he would have to go. Since that would ruin his carefully laid plans, the smart thing to do was disappear from sight.

The tiny staircase reminded him of the narrow, steep steps he'd been forced to negotiate in Holland during one of his trips to Europe. On the wall at the bottom of the stairs she'd hung her PI license, her credentials in law enforcement and her educational diplomas.

University of Utah, College of Engineering, Honorary Bachelor of Arts Degree in Computer Engineering awarded to Annabelle Lathrop Forrester.

Every time he passed them, his self-loathing increased for the cavalier way he had demanded that she give up her career for him. How blind he'd been not to see that her background, her education and experiences in the workplace contributed to the whole woman. It was all part of what made her so fascinating and irresistible to him.

In light of how ruthlessly he'd let go with the ultimatum that she give up everything to become his wife, it was nothing short of a miracle that she'd been willing to take his case now, that she was allowing him to live in her home, albeit temporarily.

Some men never got a second chance. He realized he was one of the lucky ones. Vowing not to make another fatal mistake, he entered the basement room which had come as a complete surprise the first time he'd seen it.

She'd made her downstairs into one big study furnished in creams and yellows with a couple of attractive couches, a coffee table and recessed lighting. It had been remodeled by knocking out partitions that didn't hold up the house.

The south wall contained some sophisticated electronic equipment including a phone, several computers—one of which had a camera and voice capabilities, a printer, a fax machine and a color copier. It resembled the equipment in his own study at the condo.

Another wall contained floor-to-ceiling shelves of books and historical artifacts he had enjoyed examining. On the far right was an eight-inch replica of an Olmec head found in Mexico. A row of impressive books devoted to South American archaeology lined the shelves.

Next came an Egyptian scarab placed next to a set of books on ancient hieroglyphs, the Dead Sea Scrolls and the Lakish Letters. All of it her hobby after she'd taken several student tours to Mexico and Egypt.

What he loved most were a series of framed, small colored photographs of Annabelle in desert headdress, perched on a camel, the pyramids behind her. She reminded him of a young Bedouin princess.

He'd stolen one of them because he couldn't resist, hoping she'd never notice. Maybe she already had noticed and just hadn't said anything. If that were the case, then it was the best of signs.

Obviously she spent most of her time down here. The whole atmosphere was cozy and inviting. He loved it on sight. He'd loved *her* on sight. She'd crawled right into his heart and made herself at home.

He probably shouldn't have mentioned kissing her on the heels of Caroline's departure. But something had come over him. She was in his blood. He couldn't lose her. *He refused to lose her.*

"Good night, Rand," he heard her call from the top of the stairs a few minutes later.

"Good night, Annabelle. Call me when you get a break and tell me what's happening."

"You do the same."

"I will. Drive carefully."

Everything about their relationship felt so natural. *Hell.* He felt like her husband. Territorial and protective. *Like they were married.*

He wanted Annabelle Forrester for his wife. He

wanted her to be the mother of their children. He
wanted an adorable little daughter who looked like her
mother, who had her mother's dancing curls, golden
eyes and heart-shaped mouth. He knew in his gut life
couldn't get better than that.

The more distance Annabelle put between her and the
house, the more homesick she became. Something terrible was happening to her.

*Don't kid yourself, Annabelle. Something terrible
has already happened. You're so in love with Rand
Dunbarton, you practically threw yourself in his arms
a little while ago. Don't you have any sense? Any
pride?*

Tears rolled down her cheeks.

*Rand's just playing around. Nothing's changed.
You're still the same person you were a year ago, but
he didn't want that person for his wife then, and he
doesn't want you for a wife now.*

*When the case is over, he'll be gone, out of your
life. If you succumb now, you'll be ruined forever.*

*Tomorrow you're going to have to make major
changes, starting with Rand going back to his hotel
room to live until the case is solved. No more cozy
togetherness, no more sharing. No more opportunities
to give in to temptation...*

With everything sorted out, she pulled into
Dunbarton's employee parking lot wearing a determined look on her face. What she needed to do was
concentrate on getting the job done so she could move
on to another case and forget that there was ever a
man named Rand who made her desire the impossible.

The night started out slow and never picked up. By four in the morning, Annabelle was beginning to wonder if Bryan Ludlow's sabotage spree was over when she got a call on her cellular from Rand.

"Yes?"

"We hit the jackpot."

Her adrenaline started to flow. She sat straight up in the chair. "What happened?"

"I've been calling in on the support line for hours. Twenty minutes ago, the same voice you taped answered my call. I started the trace and kept him going long enough to get a phone number.

"He tried to do the same thing to me that he tried on you. If I hadn't been on to him, he would have wiped out your hard drive. It makes you wonder how many hard drives he has ruined."

"He's a menace all right. How did you keep your cool when you knew you were talking to the teenager responsible for all your grief?"

"Believe it or not, I kind of enjoyed it. He's a bright boy. Of course I would enjoy it a lot more if I knew he was working on his own."

"I know. That part troubles me, too. What's the phone number?"

When he had given it to her she said, "I'm calling this in to the office. Someone's on duty and they'll give us a name and address. Excellent work, Rand. At the rate you're going, you'll probably have your own case solved by lunchtime and Roman will end up having to pay you!"

She thought he would laugh, or at least chuckle.

When he did neither, she didn't understand. "Rand? Are you still there?"

"Of course I am, sweetheart."

Sweetheart? Her body shook. It had been a long time since she'd heard him use that endearment with her. He sounded strange, upset, or maybe she was just tired and it was her imagination.

"I'll call you with any information as soon as I hear back from the office."

"You do that."

"I will."

Bewildered by the sudden tension, she clicked off, then called the office. Phil was on duty. She gave him the phone number and told him she would hold while he found out what he could.

While she waited, her puzzlement grew over Rand's strange behavior a few minutes ago. She would have thought he would be overjoyed they were getting closer to solving the case.

"Annie?"

"I'm here."

"The phone registration is under the name Mark J. Owens at 3990 Sundance Lane in Sandy."

"Thanks, Phil. You always do good work."

"Yeah, yeah."

"Over and out."

The name didn't ring any bells, but she knew the address. The homes in that area ranged in the $850,000 to the $1,000,000 category, set up at the base of the mountains south of Salt Lake proper.

Bryan Ludlow's home was worth a great deal more than that located in the Salt Lake Country Club area.

But whoever Bryan was hanging out with, they obviously had money, too. A professional hacker who'd once worked for Rand's company?

Without wasting any more time, she phoned Rand and told him the news. "Does the name Owens appear on that list?"

"No."

"Okay. We'll call Trina and see if she's ever heard of Mark Owens. Depending on what she says, we'll take it from there. I'll be off in an hour and drive straight home. By then Trina ought to be up and getting ready for school."

"You think she might know something?"

"Did you ever have a close girlfriend in high school?"

"No."

"That's right. You were too busy working on becoming Computer Man of the Decade."

"You make it sound like a sin."

She blinked. "I didn't mean to. I was paying you a compliment."

"Really."

"Yes, *really*." She was getting that hot and bothered feeling again.

"Did you have a close boyfriend in high school?" he fired back without missing a beat.

His question made her realize how little she and Rand had known about each other when they'd decided to get married. They'd been too caught up by excitement and desire to do much thinking at all. Now, when it was too late, they were really starting to get know what made the other person tick. The whole situation was driving her over the edge...

"No, but Janet did," Annabelle finally responded. "They told each other everything. That's probably why they broke up in college. They knew too much about each other for their own good. Her roots for becoming a good bankruptcy attorney were probably formed then."

Rand's laugh sounded cruel. "So what you're saying is, Trina probably knows Bryan inside out."

"Yes."

"For that I owe Trina and you a debt of gratitude."

"I was only doing my job."

"No. Most adults don't have time for teenagers. You didn't blow her off. You're unique, Annabelle."

I can't take much more of this.

"There's a call coming in. I have to answer it."

"Understood. Hurry home."

Stop saying that as if you mean it, Rand.

Nothing amused Rand more than to witness the way Annabelle could lie with impunity on the job when he knew her to be a guileless soul.

It was seven-thirty in the morning and she'd just gotten off the phone with Trina.

"Well, Mrs. Smith of the Reflections committee for the school district? What have we found out from Bryan's girlfriend?"

"Quite a lot."

"Let's have breakfast and you can tell me about it." He started for the dining room where he'd prepared eggs Benedict and homemade coffee cake.

"Rand?" She wasn't far behind him. "I—I'm afraid this has got to stop."

He knew exactly what she was talking about. She'd only slept in his hotel room one night. Now she was back home and they *were* living together right now. Except for the sleeping arrangements, they might as well be man and wife.

"Have I made too big a mess of your kitchen?"

An exasperated sound came out of her. "Of course not."

"If you don't like my cooking, it won't hurt my feelings."

"It's not that. I *love* your cooking."

Those words helped to calm the savage beast. "Then let's enjoy the food while it's hot."

"I should be waiting on *you* in my own home. Not the other way around."

He served her a portion of everything, then himself. "Let's get something straight, Annabelle. I've learned a lot about equality after being around you. You're out there trying to solve a big problem for me. The least I can do is make myself useful around here while you're gone. We both have to eat."

"Yes, but there's food, and then there's *food for the gods!*"

"That's the nicest compliment I've ever received."

"Well it's true. Your cooking puts mine to shame."

"So that's why you're so grumpy."

"I'm sorry." Her contrite little voice made him want to wrap her in his arms.

"Tell me what Trina had to say."

It took her a minute to answer because she had started making inroads on her eggs.

"Mark Owens is Daniel Ludlow's brother-in-law, Bryan's uncle."

Rand paused in the act of drinking his orange juice. "What an interesting twist."

"That's what I thought. Apparently he took his wife and children on a two month vacation in Europe. When they get back, Mark is going to be Daniel's campaign manager for the gubernatorial race."

"Maybe Bryan has it in for his uncle as well as his father."

"I'm worried about that, too. Trina's pretty sure Bryan broke in his aunt and uncle's house as soon as they left on their trip and has been living there without anyone having a clue. No telling what he might have gotten up to since the house has been vacated."

"Maybe his accomplice is staying there with him."

"That's what we're going to find out. How are you at washing windows?"

He smiled, already loving Plan B. "I did my fair share growing up."

"Then you're hired."

"Who are we?"

"We're Ray and Lois," she said on a definitive tone. Her talent for creating clever fronts never ceased to amaze him. "Twice a year we clean the Owens's walls, woodwork and windows."

Rand had to admit it was a brilliant plan. "When we walk in uninvited, Bryan Ludlow won't be able to question our right to be there because he isn't supposed to be on the premises himself."

"That's right." She darted him one of her impish smiles. "Of course being the teenage 'con' that he is, he'll come up with some plausible explanation why he's there. If his 'friend' is present, we'll all do a little dance around each other and get real chummy."

"I presume this project will take us several days to accomplish."

She nodded. "Trina says it's a big house."

A feeling of exultation swept through Rand. As long as the case wasn't solved, he had a reason to be underfoot day and night. He needed more time to ingratiate himself so Annabelle wouldn't ever want him to leave. What made him nervous was the speed with which she accomplished her objective.

"Does Trina know the layout?"

"Yes. She's been to a lot of their parties with Bryan. Any service people enter through a door on the side of the house. We'll start cleaning one room at a time so we can plant listening devices. I'll show you how to hide them."

Rand could only shake his head in wonder. She was almost scary the way she moved in for the kill. Would that *he* were her quarry.

"One of the guys from the office will park the mobile unit down the street from the Owens's home so he can monitor all conversations and tape them. I think that covers everything, except for my job as a night technician for Dunbarton's which is no longer a necessity."

Rand finished off the rest of coffee cake before responding.

"Don't worry about the distinction of being the

employee with the shortest work record in company history. I'll fix it with Howard as soon as I know he's in the office.''

''How?'' She gazed at him expectantly.

''I'll tell him that I was looking over the résumés of the technicians and felt that his newest employee's talents were wasted in the Salt Lake office. Then I'll explain that I phoned Mrs. Black to offer her an engineering job in the Phoenix office, and she accepted it.''

''Thank you.''

Annabelle's sheepish look was priceless.

''Speaking of jobs,'' he muttered, ''when you've solved the Ludlow case, how would you like to take on an even bigger assignment?''

Her sheepish look suddenly turned to one of bewilderment. ''What do you mean?''

Taking a calculated risk he said, ''I mean, how would you like to become the head of security for the Dunbarton Corporation?''

''You mentioned that before. I thought you were kidding.''

''Not at all,'' Rand assured her. ''You could still live in Salt Lake and work for Roman, but between cases you could commute to Phoenix where you would have your own office and staff to oversee security problems within the company. You might like the challenge as well as the change in scene.''

''You can't possibly be serious.''

''Why? You don't think you're good enough?''

She shifted her gaze to her plate.

''In case you need proof of your worth, I'll be

happy to replay the tape of your job interview with Howard.''

With her head still bent she muttered, ''Even if I thought you weren't joking, I haven't done the job I was hired to do for you yet.''

Why was her voice shaking?

He hoped it was because she was as excited as he was at the prospect of their working together once the business with Bryan Ludlow had been cleared up. At least she hadn't give him a flat-out no.

''It's only a matter of time,'' he commented mildly, ''but you don't have to give me an answer right now. I just want you to think about it.''

''Oh—there's the phone!'' she cried out as if she'd never heard one ring before. ''Excuse me a moment.'' She flew to the kitchen.

Rand cleared the table before following her. While he loaded the dishwasher, she conducted a rather hushed conversation with her back turned to him.

Luckily it was the wall phone and not her cellular, so she couldn't walk away. From the sounds of it, the call was personal. He heard the name Gerard used several times.

How important is he to you, Annabelle?

For the first time in his life Rand was hit by an attack of sheer, unadulterated jealousy, the kind Shakespeare's Othello must have felt when he thought Desdemona had been unfaithful to him.

Rand had seen the play done on numerous occasions, but he'd never understood just how destructive that emotion could be, never having been forced to deal with it before. For two cents he'd grab the phone away from Annabelle and tell *Gerard* to go take a permanent leap!

Just once she half turned, flashing Rand a look that probably said she'd like to be alone. He pretended not to see it and kept busy cleaning up the kitchen.

As soon as she hung up the receiver he said, "If that was Janet, I hope you let her know that I told you about the faxes she sent you yesterday."

"I forgot about those," she mumbled. "That was Gerard, one of the PI's."

"How come he didn't call you on your cellular?"

"Because he knows I reserve it for business."

"I'm sorry," Rand said, trying to interject the right amount of remorse in his tone. "If I had known it was personal, I wouldn't have come in. I figured that if we were going to start cleaning house later today, I'd better do your dishes first."

"It's all right, Rand."

"No, I don't think it is. Did he somehow find out I've been staying here? Has it caused complications for you? If so, I'll be happy to explain the truth to him."

In fact it would give Rand the greatest pleasure to let Gerard know exactly how things were going to stand with Annabelle from here on out.

"No. It's nothing like that. We dated some, but it's been over for quite a while."

Lord. So she *had* been involved with someone else. The knowledge hit him like a blow to his gut.

"But he didn't get the point until just now, is that it?" Rand's voice rasped.

"No. Our relationship wasn't like that."

"So how was it?"

"If you must know, he's still in love with his dead wife."

And you're in love with me, Annabelle. One of these days I'm going to get you to admit it.

The news about Gerard shouldn't have made Rand so euphoric. It sounded like he and the bereaved widower had a lot in common, the only difference being that fortunately for Rand, Annabelle was still very much alive.

"It's probably just as well that you and I have a physically taxing job before us today. Hard manual labor puts the rest of the world into the proper perspective. Do you want me to go pick up the supplies we'll need? I'll phone Howard at the same time and inform him of Mrs. Black's new status with the company."

She looked like she was in some sort of daze. He didn't think the crack female PI who made up part of Roman Lufka's renowned private investigative staff got into this state very often. As far as Rand was concerned, he would do everything in his power to keep her off balance until she caved in and came running.

"If you wouldn't mind."

"Not at all."

"Thank you. I want to shower and answer those faxes."

"Do whatever you need to do. I won't be back for at least an hour. One thing I should ask before I go. Do you want me to pick you up a pair of rubber gloves?"

By the incredulous look on her face, his question was the last thing she would ever have imagined him asking.

"I don't think so. I've never used them."

He smiled. "I just wanted to be sure. My mother never attacked her housework without them."

CHAPTER SIX

As SOON as the siren went off, Annabelle knew Rand had gone and it was safe to dash downstairs. She read Janet's faxes, both of which asked her what was going on. How come she hadn't phoned or faxed Janet back? Did it have anything to do with the P file?

The P stood for personal. It was a standing joke between them because nothing had gone on in either of their personal lives for such a long time, they both figured they would go to their graves old maids.

She turned on her computer and started typing a response. She could hardly see for the tears gushing from her eyes.

Dear J:

If you really want to know, I'm working on a case for my X-fiancé. That's right. He's in town. Take another deep breath.

And no—it's not what you think.

One day when it's not classified, I'll tell you about it. Get this... He's offered me the job of the century in Phoenix. Head of security. My own office. My own staff.

A child could figure out that he stopped seeing me as wife material a long time ago. I suppose I should be flattered that the Computer Man of the Year has decided my career isn't so negligible after all, and can be put to some practical use.

Which goes to show he never understood me, otherwise he would realize head of security is not the position I had in mind. As of today, I'm permanently deleting the P file.

Love, A.

Since Rand had gone to the store in the rental car and all their equipment was in the back seat and trunk, he ended up driving them to the Owens's house. En route, Annabelle showed him one of the listening devices and explained how to install it.

When they arrived at their destination at the south end of the valley, they discovered a large, attractive two-story mock-Tudor home. It was nestled in the foothills, partially hidden from the street by heavy foliage.

To gain entrance, they had to pass through a locked, wrought-iron gate. Annabelle used her master key to let them in, then Rand proceeded up the drive through the dense scrub oak.

Part of the private road veered to the right to form a circle at the front entrance. The other part ran along the side of the house and around the back where they could see a three car garage.

There was no sign of life.

At the side entrance Trina had alluded to, Rand pulled to a stop and shut off the ignition. "All right," he said, turning in his seat to look at her. "We've come this far. Now what?"

Rand was such a natural at everything he did, she found it almost impossible to remember that he hadn't always been one of Roman's PI's. If she weren't so in love with him, she would be having the time of her life.

Avoiding his eyes she said, "We play it by ear from here on out. I'll get us through the door and then we'll start bringing in the equipment. The mobile unit will be along shortly disguised as a furniture delivery van."

When his mouth curved into that smile which melted her bones, she couldn't focus on anything. That never happened with a colleague. But therein lay the danger because Rand Dunbarton wasn't a colleague. He was a breathtaking male. Despite the pain of the past, her desire, her love for him was stronger than ever.

She didn't know how it had happened, but he seemed to have changed over the last year. It was Rand, but a different Rand. More laid-back. Mellow.

Living underfoot made him seem an integral part of her. Waking, sleeping, he was there haunting her, making her ache for all the things a woman in love wanted and needed from the man of her dreams.

He *was* the man of her dreams.

Her child's world had been full of castles and princesses. Though she'd grown into a woman, her idealism hadn't changed. The only difference now was that her dark-haired prince with the blindingly blue eyes had a recognizable face and wore modern day clothing. He was sitting next to her. If she reached out her hand, she could touch him.

"Let's go," she murmured. "We'll just speak in our natural voices and see what happens."

They both got out of the car at the same time. Rand's eyes met hers over the roof. "I'm having so much fun, maybe I'll ask Roman for a part-time job. Of course I'll need references. If I don't bungle this assignment too badly, maybe I can get you to put in a good word for me."

"I'd be happy to." Though she'd put on her brightest voice, she groaned inwardly. When she thought about it, Annabelle couldn't imagine anything more wonderful than being married to Rand, and living and working in Salt Lake with him. But that kind of dreaming only led to more heartache.

His compelling mouth curved upward, as if he could read her mind. *Damn.* "Where do you want to start, *Lois?*"

Dressed in a white T-shirt and jeans like herself, he followed her into the house carrying the stepladder and their supplies as if this were an everyday occurrence. She had to take another breath because the sight of him thrilled her too much.

He provided cover while she plugged a touch-tone decoder into the kitchen phone, then installed a CCD camera with audio camouflaged as a wall plate into an electrical outlet. The listening capability picked up conversation and transmitted it to the van parked down the street.

When she was finished she said, "I think we'll tackle the living room first, since it's the biggest job. If you'll help me move the furniture away from the walls, I'll begin cleaning while you attack the windows."

"Sounds good to me."

Arms loaded, they walked through several rooms to the traditionally furnished living room, a long rectangle with cove moldings and wainscoting throughout. Resting their things on the carpet, Annabelle bent down to install another camera with listening device in one of the outlets.

"How about a little music?" Rand produced a small boom box he'd purchased along with their equipment and turned it on to a popular rock station.

"Pure genius," she mouthed the words at him. If Bryan were in the house, he would know it had been invaded by someone other than his aunt and uncle.

"We try," he mouthed back with a wink.

She immediately bent over to pour the liquid cleaner into a bucket, but too late, she'd already reacted to his potent charm. Her heart had already received its jolt for the morning just being around him like this, and she would never be the same again.

Out of the corner of her eye she watched him get busy on the mullioned windows. He worked with effortless male grace. She marveled at his ability to adapt to any situation. A person could be forgiven for thinking he cleaned houses for a living and enjoyed it. She could stare at him for hours and derive the greatest pleasu—

"Who are you guys?" a young man's voice sounded in the room, jarring Annabelle from her fantasies. She almost dropped the sponge mop.

"Hi!" She smiled at him. "I'm Lois and this is Ray. We didn't know your parents left any of you home from their European trip. Which one are you?"

Thanks to the pictures and information Trina had

fed Annabelle, she not only recognized him as Bryan Ludlow, she'd learned enough background on the Owens family to bluff her way through this first meeting.

"I'm not a relation. My name's Kevin. I live down the street. The Owens pay me to house-sit." The tall, lanky, nice-looking blond teen dressed in sweats and a polo shirt lied without betraying the slightest sign of nervousness. "How did you get in?"

Rand must have heard the aggressiveness in the young man's tone. He turned down the music and straightened to his full, intimidating height. No man of Annabelle's acquaintance had a more authoritative presence than Rand whose protective instincts appeared to have come to the fore and were on full alert.

"Probably the same way you did," he insinuated silkily. Annabelle actually felt kind of sorry for Bryan whose belligerent demeanor vanished immediately in the face of such unquestioned male dominance. "My wife and I clean this place twice a year."

Wife?

Annabelle lowered the sponge end of the mop into the pail to cover her shock.

"Are you going to be here long?" There was a conciliatory change in Bryan's attitude now.

"Probably two days. The Owens are going to put on a big political fund-raiser dinner when they get back, so we've been asked to give the place a thorough cleaning."

The mention of that kind of a dinner lent veracity to Rand's words, inflicting another chink in Bryan's armor. His brown eyes slid away from Rand who'd gone back to the windows to clean them.

"If the music is bothering you, we'll turn it off," Annabelle volunteered brightly.

"Hey—" He spread his hands apart. "No problem. It's cool that guys your age listen to metal."

"Yeah?" Rand grinned at him. "I was a guitarist with a rock band in high school. Lois was our drummer. Guess we never outgrew our love for it."

Annabelle gulped.

"That's awesome," Bryan enthused. "Do you guys have kids?"

"Not yet, but we're working on it, aren't we, sweetheart."

She mumbled something incoherent and kept doing the walls with the mop.

"They'll be lucky."

"You think?" she interjected.

"Yeah. They'll be able to play the kind of music they want and not get grounded for it."

"Do you know who Mozart is, Kevin?"

"Heck, yes. I've had to take piano lessons since I was six. I hated them. Last year I quit. My parents went berserk!"

"You want to know something funny?" she confided.

"What?" By now he'd plunked himself on an Italian provincial chair with legs stretched out in front of him, obviously lonely for a little company and happy to have someone to talk to.

"My dad asked me not to play Mozart's Requiem Mass when he was in the house."

"You're kidding!"

"No. He said it was too sad. After my mom died he couldn't listen to anything classical. That's why he didn't mind rock or metal."

"That's amazing. My parents won't let me listen to anything but classical at home." He looked up at her intently. "You love classical?"

She nodded. "I do. When I was a lot younger, I'd go down the basement, put on my headphones to listen to it, then I'd play around on my computer which I loved as much as my music."

He sat forward. "I love computers, too."

"She's *really* into them," Rand offered, having finished up one set of windows and starting on another. "Sometimes I accuse her of loving her Tronimania 500 more than she loves me."

"You have a Tronimania?" Kevin's mocking laughter filled the room.

She moved her pail along the floorboard to a new section of wall to wash. "Don't knock it. That computer has all the latest stuff for a one man band. When I hook up the amplifiers, I can practice my drums and feel like I'm with the old group again."

Rand paused between panes. "What kind of a computer do you have, Kevin?"

"I own a half dozen different kinds, but I've torn the motherboards apart and have rebuilt my own computer."

Annabelle shook her head. "I don't even know what a motherboard is. How did you learn to do things like that?"

"I don't know." He shrugged his shoulders. "My

parents gave me a Dunbarton when I was twelve. I really liked it and read all the literature. Pretty soon I was turned on to computers big time. Now when I need to repair something, I just buy old parts and fix them and everything works.''

"You remind me of that teenager in *WarGames*. Did you ever see that movie?''

"Sure. Everybody has.''

"Except nobody could really do the things he did in that show,'' Annabelle baited him, then scooted her stuff down the room a few more feet.

Bryan followed her. "What do you mean?''

"Breaking in on big computer systems, decoding security devices. It's a great story for the movie audience, but it doesn't happen in real life.''

"Sure it does.''

Behind Bryan's shoulder, Annabelle could see Rand giving her the thumbs-up signal. "Kevin's right, sweetheart. It happens.''

She schooled herself not to react to Rand's endearment. In a quiet aside to Bryan she said, "I'm afraid my husband believes everything he sees on television.''

"I heard that.'' To her surprise, Rand closed the distance between them and kissed her on the neck. A river of molten heat ran through her body making it throb.

"Don't you remember that article in *Time* magazine?'' he murmured against her skin. "The one about the sixteen-year-old kid who broke into the main computer at a brokerage firm from his own house and made thousands of dollars buying and selling stock?''

The touch of his lips left her trembling and vulnerable. He distracted her until she couldn't think clearly. Their teenage interloper was clearly enjoying the byplay.

"How could he do that without a password of some kind?" At this point she only had one more section of wall to finish cleaning. Rand started on another batch of windows at her end. Bryan stuck to them like glue.

"He got it by running someone's program from a local server and learning the password. Apparently the police caught up with him and he went to prison."

"That's horrible."

"That kid was stupid," Bryan blurted.

Rand's eyes sent Annabelle a private message before he switched his attention to the teen. "What do you mean?"

"The guy you were talking about had to break in on another program to figure it out which was a dumb thing to do, a dead giveaway."

"If it had been you, how would you have done it?" Rand asked in a nonchalant manner. Annabelle held her breath, waiting for Bryan's answer.

"Easy. I'd just make friends with somebody whose sister or brother worked for the company and get them to slip me the password. That way no one could trace anything."

So *that* was how Bryan had broken in on Rand's technical line. *He didn't have an accomplice.* Annabelle imagined Rand was feeling a great sense of relief about now. So was she.

"I can see a family member getting that kind of

information out of another family member, Kevin, but I can't see that person giving it to you or anyone else.''

"They would for enough money, like a thousand dollars.''

Good grief. Only someone like Bryan could bribe a friend with that kind of incentive.

Rand nodded. "Yes, I guess a friend your age would probably do anything for that kind of money.''

"Yup.''

"That's interesting. From a purely monetary aspect of course. What is sad is that the kid who went to prison had never been taught that it's morally wrong to hack.''

"Morally?" Bryan sounded impatient.

"Of course. Hackers don't know about the costs associated with their actions. Most kids are too young to realize the full ramifications. That teenager didn't own any property or have a job. He didn't have any idea of what it means to be responsible or care about anyone but himself.

"Not only didn't he consider that it was a federal offense to steal money, he ruined hundreds of programs, caused the loss of data which cost the company millions of dollars.''

"My dad says that every big business builds a loss factor into their operating budget. It's the price of doing business.''

Bryan Ludlow might be a brainy child, but he had developed a self-serving attitude to justify his actions.

Annabelle finished the last section of wall, then walked over to the teen with her mop. "You mean like a supermarket that expects four percent of its merchandise to be stolen per fiscal year and they just have to deal with it?''

"Yeah. Exactly. I mean, if the company has bad security, then that's their problem."

"What if it were *your* company, Kevin?"

He flashed her a self-satisfied smile. "One day I'm going to own a computer business and no one will ever be able to rip me off because I'll have a foolproof system."

Annabelle winked at Bryan. "Didn't you know there's no such a thing as a foolproof system?"

"*Mine* will be."

"I think that's what the kid said to the judge before he was sentenced," Rand informed him. "Well, sweetheart? We're finished in here. What do you say we put the furniture back in place, then go out for a hamburger?''

"That sounds good. You want to come to lunch with us, Kevin?"

After a slight hesitation, "No thanks, but maybe if I give you some money you could bring me back a couple of double cheeseburgers with everything and some fries? I'm supposed to be here all the time."

"You mean you never go out?"

"Well, sure. My folks come over and do my job for me when I need a break. The thing is, I'm saving all the money I can and the Owens are depending on me to do a good job. Besides bringing in the mail and watering plants, I'm supposed to hang around as much as possible to be on the lookout for intruders. If you want to leave now, I'll put everything back."

"Thanks, but that's our job."

"No, really! I haven't got anything else to do. Just let me run and get some change."

"If you're sure."

He nodded.

"Okay. We'll meet you at the car then." Without warning Rand slid his hands onto Annabelle's shoulders from behind. "Come with me, Mrs. Adams."

Mrs. Adams?

"Don't you think you're overdoing it just a little bit?" she complained as they started down the length of the room with his arm around her shoulders.

When they reached the French doors he murmured, "I haven't even gotten started yet." Suddenly the room tilted. She found herself engulfed in a powerful pair of arms, then Rand's dark head was descending.

Unable to help himself, he covered her mouth with his own. He'd been insane with wanting to taste it again.

She wasn't fighting him, but she wasn't exactly meeting him halfway, either. Maybe it was the distance between them causing the trouble. If he evened the odds...

Wrapping his arms more tightly around her, he picked her up so her feet were off the ground and brought her head level with his. Then he deepened their kiss.

A little muffled gasp escaped her throat before her mouth opened to him completely the way it used to do.

Suddenly Rand wasn't in control of the situation. Their kiss had taken on a life of its own. Like a mighty river, the blood rushed through his veins. When he'd first kissed her a year ago, he had no idea a woman's mouth could give a man so much pleasure. Not just any woman's mouth. *Annabelle's.*

More moaning sounds escaped her throat, igniting new fires. He lengthened their kiss, aware that the desire to lower them both to the floor and remove their clothes was growing into a raging need. Rand was fast reaching that dangerous point of no return.

"I—I think you'd better put me d-down," she stammered when he finally allowed her to take a breath. It sounded more like a desperate plea. Her body was trembling, just like his.

Both of them were on the verge of being swept away. He could ignore her weak supplication, or he could do the gentlemanly thing. If he let her go, they would both suffer deprivation. To do what his body was screaming for him to do would bring them rapture because he knew she wanted it as much as he did.

But afterward, she might despise him for moving everything ahead too fast. They were just starting to get to really know each other. But not enough time had passed for her to fully trust him yet.

Struggling against his own nature, he slowly lowered her to the floor. She averted her eyes and backed away from him.

"Do you know," Rand began in a voice that sounded oddly husky even to his own ears, "you have the most delectable mouth. I think I have to have another taste of it."

So saying he captured her lips once more, never wanting to stop drinking from her sweetness.

"Whoa. You guys are worse than some of the couples on the soap operas."

Rand finally lifted his head. He had no idea he and Annabelle had had an audience. What they'd experienced just now was private and sacred. Annabelle's cheeks were scarlet.

"That's because we're still on our honeymoon."

"You're kidding! How long have you been married?"

"Five years," he called over his shoulder as he ushered a subdued Annabelle through the rest of the house and out the door to the driveway.

As he opened the passenger door of the rental car so she could get in, she whispered panic-stricken, "Don't forget that Phil is out in the surveillance van and can hear everything we're saying."

Obviously she was embarrassed, but he didn't particularly care. Her eyes revealed she'd been dazed by their passion. He'd seen her in this state many times before when they'd been dating in Phoenix. She sort of fell on the seat, limp. The magic was still there, stronger than ever. He would do whatever it took to get her back.

"You guys are awesome."

Rand shut the door after her, then took the money from Bryan. "We're not so different from any other happily married couple."

Bryan dogged Rand's footsteps around to the driver's side of the car. "I never see my parents kiss like that."

"How do you know they weren't like Lois and me when they were first married?"

"I guess I don't. But you guys will probably act like this even when you have kids."

"I'm planning on it," Rand vowed, "but everyone shows their feelings differently, Kevin. Just remember how lucky you are that your parents decided to have *you*." He got in the car and talked to Bryan through the open window.

The teen actually blushed. "Well, yeah. But you know what I mean."

"Ray's right, you know." Annabelle finally found her voice. It, too, sounded low and husky. "And when you think about it, I haven't heard of very many kids who are given a Dunbarton computer at the age of twelve, let alone expensive piano lessons for all the years you were growing up. You ought to be counting your blessings. My mom died giving birth to me. I envy you having both parents around."

He averted his eyes.

"Do you have a girlfriend, Kevin?" Rand asked casually before he started the ignition.

"Yeah."

"Someone special?"

"Yeah. Trina and I have been going together a couple of years and plan to get married someday."

As Rand fastened his seat belt, he decided the two teens must really care about each other, otherwise Trina wouldn't have been so desperate to trace Bryan and help him stay out of trouble.

"We can relate, can't we, Lois?" Rand pulled Annabelle next to him on the seat and kept his hand on her thigh. It was an intimate gesture. He knew she wanted to push it away, but didn't dare with Bryan looking on.

"Picture this, Kevin— There I was talking with my buddies in the high school parking lot when this great-looking redhead in a Jeep roared into an empty space, her cat's eyes glowing. We all stood there in breathless anticipation waiting for her to get out. You know what I mean?"

"Yeah—" Bryan's smile had widened into a huge grin.

"When she did, all I can say is, it was well worth the wait."

"I agree," Bryan offered boldly.

It was Annabelle's turn to go all shades of red.

"That's when I decided that one day my pocket Venus would be my wife!"

"*Ray!*"

Bryan laughed his head off. "You really call her your pocket Venus? That's perfect!"

Rand's eyes made a slow appraisal of her face and figure. "She *is* pretty perfect, isn't she."

There was fire in her eyes now.

"I think we'd better get going, Ray. We've got half the main floor to clean after lunch."

"You're right." With great reluctance he removed his hand and started to back down the driveway to the part where they could turn around. "See you in a little while, Kevin."

The teen waved them off. Annabelle waved back before moving as far away from Rand as possible.

"Your case is practically solved, Mr. Dunbarton. All we have to do is find out from Trina which friend of Bryan's has recently come into a lot of money and we'll know which older brother or sister inadvertently gave out the security password.''

"It's scary how clever you are, sweetheart,'' he mocked.

She kept her head turned away from him. "I think I'll wait to phone Trina until she's home from school. My PTA *persona* might not go over a third time.''

"Now that I know our boy genius isn't working with a professional, we can both afford to relax a little. Come on back over here.'' He patted the empty space between them.

"You can stop the act now, Rand.''

"What act? You told me to play this by ear. That's what I've been doing.''

"But it wasn't nece—''

"I beg to differ,'' he said in a slightly sterner tone. "Without the right approach, butter wouldn't have melted in that kid's mouth. Thinking we're a lovey-dovey couple has taken him completely off his guard.''

CHAPTER SEVEN

ANNABELLE'S heart thudded from too much adrenaline. *Your ploy may have fooled Bryan, but it has practically destroyed me.*

"I'll open the gate," she volunteered, practically leaping from the car to get away from him long enough to suck fresh air in her lungs.

As soon as she got back in the car, Rand turned to the left and they drove down the street past the surveillance van. Phil gave her the victory sign.

"What exactly did that signify, Annabelle?"

"That he's picking up sound and apparently it's very informative."

"Maybe Bryan's friend is hiding upstairs or down in the basement."

"When he ordered two double cheeseburgers, I wondered the same thing."

"Except that I used to eat two of everything for every meal at his age."

"But you're a much bigger man than Bryan."

"You noticed."

"I noticed," she said before she could stop herself. "When I first met you in Phoenix, I couldn't believe you were the head of Dunbarton's. I thought you were a lineman for the Green Bay Packers."

"Why not the Denver Broncos?"

She bowed her head, afraid to look at him. "My

dad loved Coach Vince Lombardi, so I guess it was the first team that came to my mind."

"I'm not complaining."

"Did you play football?"

"I did, but not after high school."

"Were you an all-stater?"

"Yes."

"Could you have gone on to play college ball?"

"Yes, but my real interest lay in another direction."

"Obviously."

He cocked his head. "It's true I've always enjoyed the computer scene, but I'm talking about my love of history. After mother died, I hitchhiked through Europe with a couple of my buddies. We saw and did it all. I didn't want to stop there. I would have liked to have gone on to Africa...

"But my dad needed me, and I realized there wasn't anything I could do with a doctorate in foreign travel. So this rolling stone came home and I worked my way up in Dad's company while I attended college courses at night."

"I was bitten by the same bug," she admitted. "At one point I told my dad I wanted to become a tour guide for a travel company overseas. That's when he sat me down and told me about the time he wanted to buy a boat and sail around the world."

Rand chuckled. "I guess we didn't end up too poorly, did we."

"Speak for yourself. I live hand-to-mouth in a pillbox."

"At least your charming pillbox is your own. If

you'd followed your dreams, your world would be the inside of a tour bus whose air conditioning unit never works during the hottest months of the tourist season.''

She smiled in remembrance. ''Those tour buses were awful.''

''So were the broken down rental bikes and overcrowded youth hostels.''

When her cellular phone rang, the sound startled her. She'd been so carried away by her conversation with Rand, she'd forgotten they were on a case.

''Yes?''

''It's me, Phil. Remember?''

A hot flash swept over her body. ''I—I was just about to call you.''

''Sure you were.''

''What have you learned?''

''As soon as your car left the driveway, the phone decoder picked up a bunch of Salt Lake numbers calling in on the line. An answering machine that says, 'You have reached the Dunbarton Support line,' puts them on hold.''

''Just a minute, Phil.'' Annabelle repeated to Rand what the other man told her.

Rand shook his head in exasperation. ''That little devil. He makes the poor customers wait for hours, then methodically ruins their hard drives. We've got him nailed right now, but we need to know who gave him the password to break into the system administrator and get past security before we call a halt.''

''I agree.'' She put the phone to her ear once more.

"Phil? Is there any indication that someone is in the house with him?"

"No."

"Okay. We're going to get some lunch, then head back to the house."

"Make sure it's the Owens's house and not another person's I know about."

"What do you mean?"

"You know exactly what I mean. Gerard is in mourning because he just found out you've been living with your latest client."

She turned as far away from Rand as possible. Covering the mouthpiece she hissed, "We're on a job, Phil."

"Since when do you allow a client those kinds of privileges? The guys have all driven by your house and have seen his rental car out front for the last couple of days and *nights*."

Annabelle's eyes rounded in shock.

"Rand Dunbarton has cornered you in your own lair, Annie baby. We all used to think it couldn't be done, but we underestimated his technique. That's quite a coup. Lady PI snared by computer giant in latest takeover scheme."

A prickling broke out on her face and neck. "I don't know where you get your information but—"

"Where else but the boss!"

Not Roman!

"Besides, you forget—I can hear you guys! The whole office has bets on how long you'll last with the agency."

"I'm hanging up."

"I get it. Your lord and master is tired of sharing you. Over and out."

"Anything wrong?" Rand asked in a low, velvety voice.

Her chin lifted a little higher. *Yes. Everyone is making false assumptions about you and me. Little do they know you've been playing around with my emotions, and the only offer you've extended me is the one I don't want.*

"No. Of course not."

"Like hell there isn't. Your face has a becoming blush, the price of being a beautiful redhead."

Why do you keep it up, Rand?

"When Phil's on duty, he loves to tell off-color jokes to shock people. Now, if you'll turn at the next corner, there's a Sally's Drive-In. We can get hamburgers there."

Rand followed her directions and within minutes they had arrived and placed some takeout orders. "I can hear Plan C brewing. Want to let me in on it while we wait?"

Normally Rand had an uncanny ability to read her mind. But for once, her thoughts had nothing to do with the case and everything to do with the man whose nearness and warmth was driving her crazy with needs he'd aroused back at the house.

She shouldn't have let the scene in the hotel room with Caroline provide her an excuse to move back home before she'd solved the case. But where Rand was concerned, she had no willpower at all.

"Actually, I was thinking about Bryan's motives."

"You mean to embarrass his father."

She nodded.

"I think you were right in your first assessment about him, Annabelle. He's a super-bright kid who is upset with his parents over some pretty typical teenage complaints."

"He doesn't seem sinister to me."

Rand shook his head. "No. Just misguided, and somewhat arrogant. He thinks he wants to get caught, but he has no comprehension of what would be involved if he were criminally prosecuted."

"I was thinking that since you're the person who would be bringing formal charges against him, you mi—"

"I'm way ahead of you, sweetheart," he interrupted her. "Once we establish who fed him the password, Bryan and I will have a little chat, one-on-one, about the realities of his precarious situation. With some incentives and a feasible plan of restitution, he might decide life with his parents isn't so bad."

"That's very generous of you, Rand."

You've just given me another reason to be madly in love with you. I wish to heaven I weren't.

This case needs to be solved today.

You need to go back to Phoenix.

I need...

"The dining room windows are done. Where do you want to clean next, my love?"

My love was a new endearment of Rand's. Annabelle had promised herself she wouldn't react, but it was impossible not to when she was so deeply in love with him.

With a quick glance at her watch she said, "We've got the kitchen and the den to do. Why don't we call it a day and finish those two rooms tomorrow."

"Don't you have to clean the upstairs?" Bryan's question sounded like he was actually disappointed. After eating lunch together, he'd been a captive audience all afternoon. More and more Annabelle was convinced that he and his parents needed to sit down and reopen the lines of communication.

"Not for six more months, Kevin."

By now Bryan had anticipated her needs and willingly helped carry her supplies to the walnut-paneled study. Rand's eyes darted her a private message that told her to check out the desk.

She could see in a glance what had caught his interest. There were two Dunbarton computers sitting side by side. One of them had additional boxes of memory.

"It looks like the Owens have acquired more electronic equipment since we last cleaned this room, sweetheart."

"It's no wonder. Being Daniel Ludlow's campaign manager means keeping track of thousands of financial donations and names of volunteers. I get tired just thinking about all the hours hardworking friends and relatives like the Owens spend to get decent people into politics."

Bryan's face seemed to have lost some of its color. "You think Daniel Ludlow is decent?"

"Of course." She flashed him a friendly smile. "He's a self-made man. I admire anyone who has built a business from scratch with good, hard, honest work. I plan on voting for him."

"So do I," Rand concurred. "His roots go back to the pioneers who came to Utah and settled here. A lot of wealthy men have left the state and invested their money elsewhere. Daniel Ludlow has stayed put and given millions to build the economy."

Annabelle had no idea how Rand knew so much about Bryan's father, but she should have learned long before now never to underestimate him.

While she wiped down the paneling she said, "Just the other day I saw that he chartered a 747 to bring home a Mormon missionary who'd been shot in some remote area of Peru. The young man would have died if he couldn't have been rushed to a hospital here."

"I read that same article, honey. Mr. Ludlow arranged for a Support-Flight helicopter to be waiting at Salt Lake International Airport to transport the young man to the hospital and I hear he's been paying all the bills because the family couldn't afford it."

She shook her head. "If I had his money, I'd like to think I would be the kind of person to come to someone else's rescue."

"Would that we were all as benevolent and altruistic. He's pretty amazing. As far as I'm concerned, he'll make a good governor, maybe even a great one," Rand stated unequivocally.

While they finished their work and discussed the virtues of various people in Utah politics, Bryan remained uncharacteristically silent. Something of significance was going on inside of him. It was time to leave.

"I guess we can call it a day."

"I'll tell you what," Rand murmured, "since you've done so much backbreaking labor, I'll carry everything to the kitchen. You go on out to the car and take a rest."

As usual, he could read her mind. He knew she wanted to call Trina and get the ball rolling. She was on the verge of thanking him when he added, "Tonight, Mrs. Adams, you're in for the treat of your life. I'm planning to give you one of my special back-rubs."

Intimate pictures of the two of them together rendered her breathless—a condition which was fast becoming chronic when she was around him. Once again Rand had reduced everything to the personal and put her in a position where she was forced to respond for Bryan's sake.

"Since you're older than I am, *darling*, I think maybe you're the one who is going to need the extra attention, but I won't say no to your offer to clean everything up here."

A slumberous look entered his blue eyes, turning her body molten. "Did you hear that, Kevin? My wife's going to give me special attention tonight."

Annabelle didn't wait to hear Bryan's reaction. She sped from the room hot-faced, needing to get away from Rand. Before he could join her in the car, she would phone the office and ask Roman to assign her to extra duty tonight. She didn't care what it was as long as it made things impossible for her and Rand to be together for the next eighteen hours.

Two minutes later she reached Diana on her cellular

phone and asked to speak to Roman. When Annabelle found out her boss was on a case, she left word for him to call her on his cellular. It was an emergency.

By the time Rand came out to the car, she had made her call to Trina, as well.

"We're going to meet Trina at the convenience store near her house in a few minutes," she announced as he levered himself behind the wheel. "Head toward the freeway, then take the Twenty-Third East exit. It's at the stoplight on Thirty-Third South."

"What's the hurry?" he murmured as he backed them around and headed for the gate once more.

She gritted her teeth. "Surely the answer is obvious. The sooner we get all the facts, the sooner you can stop Bryan from hurting your business, and the less money you'll have to pay the Lufka agency for our services."

It might have been her imagination but she thought they pulled out of the driveway a little too fast after she'd closed the gate and locked it.

Grabbing for her cellular phone so she wouldn't have to make conversation with him, she called Janet who was always good for a backup plan when all else failed.

Maybe the Fates were with her because for once, Janet was in her office rather than at court.

"Hi!"

"I just got your fax. We need to talk, Annie girl."

Ignoring her friend's comment Annabelle said, "What time is your dinner party tonight? I'm finishing up a case but I should be home to get ready within a couple of hours.''

"What are you tal— Oh, I get it. You're not alone. Okay. Let's see. Cocktails at seven.''

"Cocktails at seven. I'll be there.''

"Mind if I say hello to Janet?'' Rand had already reached for the phone. *He didn't believe Janet was on the other end.*

"Just a minute, Janet. Someone wants to talk to you.'' Full of confidence, she let Rand take it.

Rand could sense Annabelle was ready to bolt, but he wasn't about to let that happen. "Hello?''

"Hi!'' came a cheery female voice. Rand didn't know what to think. Maybe Annabelle really had called up her best friend. Maybe there really was a party she'd been invited to. *Without him.*

"Is this the famous bankruptcy attorney who spends her vacation in Florida reading transcripts of the Watergate trial, strictly for fun?''

He heard laughter coming from the other end. "My secret is out. Could this possibly be the voice of *Today's Fortune*'s Computer Man of the Year? Were you really a lineman for the Green Bay Packers before you went into business?''

Relief made Rand's body sag against the car seat. One thing he'd learned about Annabelle. She was an intensely private person. Nothing could have pleased him more than to know she'd been talking about him to her best friend.

"I'll answer that question if you'll answer one for me.''

"What question is that?''

"How do you make money wh—"

"When my clients don't have any?" She anticipated the rest of his words. Rand chuckled. Janet was
almost as entertaining as Annabelle. "Annabelle tells
me you just bought a new Mercedes. I'm waiting for
the answer with baited breath."

"I heard baited breath can be fatal so we'd better
not let that condition of yours go on too long."

Rand's chuckle turned into laughter. He couldn't
wait to meet Janet.

"Why don't you come by the house with Annabelle
this evening and I'll tell you."

"You're sure I won't be imposing?" By now his
gaze had swerved to the gorgeous female at his side.
She was not amused. That was too bad because he
had no intention of going away.

"With every journalist in America wanting a piece
of you and I've just been given exclusive rights to
pick your brains? Are you kidding?"

His mouth turned up at the corners. "You're thinking of the wrong man, but your kind words are nice
to hear at the end of a long working day. Annabelle
has really put us through the paces."

"I don't doubt it. She says she's been working on
a case for you. What disguise did she dream up today?"

Rand couldn't stop chuckling. "Today we were the
loving husband and wife housecleaning team of Ray
and Lois Adams."

"Give me the phone, Rand!"

Like lightning, Annabelle pulled the cellular away

from him and told Janet she would have to call her back.

The timing couldn't have been more perfect because the convenience store came into view. Rand spotted several people milling about in front. "The blond girl must be Trina. Am I right?"

"Like I said," she answered in a wooden voice, "you should be working for the CIA."

"You sound grumpy," he commented as she started to get out of the car. "I'll buy you something to eat. That ought to hold you until we get to the cocktail party."

Without commenting on anything, she marched right over to Bryan Ludlow's girlfriend and urged her to walk to the edge of the grass where they could be private. Rand followed.

"Trina? This is Ray. He's helping me on this case."

"Hello, Trina."

"Hi."

"We've just learned that Bryan has a friend whose brother or sister works for Dunbarton's in Salt Lake in some capacity. He paid that friend a thousand dollars to get the password to break in."

"I can't believe he'd do anything so stupid," Trina moaned.

"Can you think of any of Bryan's friends who've come into a lot of money in the last two weeks?"

Trina frowned. "Not really."

"Maybe it's not a friend, only an acquaintance. Someone who suddenly might have bought a really

fabulous stereo or magged out tires, a lift, search
lights for a Jeep or a Blazer—"

"Or a used motorcycle or car," Rand added.

She shook her head. "I don't know."

"That's okay," Annabelle assured her. "Just think
about it and if you come up with a name, call me. I'll
give you my cellular phone number."

While she was writing it on a piece of paper, Trina
made a sound. "Paul Iverson— I saw him riding a
brand new motorbike out of Food King's parking lot
yesterday. He works there as a grocery bagger."

"Is he a friend of Bryan's?"

"Not really, but in summer he also mows lawns
with a crew that does Mr. Ludlow's yard. Sometimes
when I'm over there swimming with Bryan, we talk
to Paul."

"Do you think the motorbike is a recent purchase?"

"Actually I thought he must have borrowed somebody's because he doesn't have a lot of money and
has always ridden his dirt bike everywhere."

"I'm going to the car to phone Howard. Keep Trina
here. I'll be right back," he whispered in Annabelle's
ear before heading in the direction of the Ford.

Using his cellular, he called in to his company and
got Howard out of a meeting. When Rand asked if
any of the technicians were named Iverson, Howard
immediately confirmed that a Barrett Iverson was em-
ployed on the day shift and had been with the company four years. That was all Rand needed to hear.

"Ask Iverson to step into your office. Don't tell
him what it's about. I'll be there within twenty

minutes." He clicked off and went in search of Annabelle who had her arm around a weeping Trina. At his approach, Annabelle lifted her head. Her questing gaze collided with Rand's. "His name is Barrett Iverson," he murmured.

Annabelle looked back at Trina. "We have good news. Ray has made a positive identification. Paul Iverson does have a brother who works for Dunbarton's. By tonight Bryan will be back home with his family and this whole situation will be cleared up."

"But Bryan's done something criminal!" The girl half sobbed the words.

"Yes, he has," Rand replied for Annabelle. "However, this is his first offense, and his motives stemmed from the desire to hurt his parents rather than from true malice of forethought against Dunbarton's. The owner of the company will probably work out some kind of a deal so it doesn't embarrass his parents or put him in jail."

"You think?" she cried out for joy.

"I can pretty well guarantee it."

"Oh, thank you." She hugged Annabelle, then Rand.

"You go on home, Trina. I can guarantee you'll hear from Bryan by tomorrow."

"Here. I've been doing a lot of baby-sitting." She extended her hand to Annabelle. It held four fifty-dollar bills. "I hired you to help find Bryan and get him to come home. Please take it." She sniffed, trying to fight the tears.

Rand was moved by the girl's sincerity and determination. Bryan Ludlow didn't know how fortunate he was. In fact the troubled teen didn't seem to have a clue about much of anything, particularly Annabelle's remarkable talent for detective work.

"Keep your money, Trina."

"But—"

"No buts. I'm going to let you in on a little secret. Bryan's parents hired my boss to find Bryan. When I told him I was already working on the case because of you, he said my part would have to be one of an unofficial capacity. When it's unofficial, I can't accept money. So keep it and enjoy."

Trina looked incredulous. "You really *can't* take my money?"

"Nope."

"But that's not fair. You've done all this work!"

"But don't you see? I've solved the problem for my boss and he pays me very well, so don't you worry about it."

"I think you're wonderful, Ms. Forrester."

"The feeling's mutual, Trina. Bryan Ludlow is a very lucky guy to have a girlfriend as caring as you."

"I agree," Rand concurred. "Any young woman who would go to the extremes you did to find your boyfriend and protect him for his own good, deserves all the best in life."

"Thanks." Her cheeks filled with color.

As soon as Trina walked off, Rand accompanied Annabelle to his rental car. "Howard has Barrett Iverson waiting in his office. When we get there, we'll phone his brother, Paul, and ask him to join us. Once that's out of the way, we'll head over to the Owens's house and speak a few home truths to Bryan.''

She nodded. ''I can see that this is going to take the rest of the night. I'd better phone Janet. She's expecting me.''

''*Us*, you mean.'' Annabelle had gotten herself in trouble on that one. ''Tell her we'll come over tomorrow night instead, if it's convenient.''

Her well-shaped head jerked around. ''Your case has been solved! You'll be back in your Phoenix office by tomorrow afternoon.''

CHAPTER EIGHT

THAT may be your plan, darling, but it's certainly not mine.

"I have no idea when I'll be returning to Arizona. For a while I'll be supervising Bryan's restitution plan for all the damage he's done."

"What do you mean?" Her voice was shaking. It pleased him no end that his news had the power to affect her so strongly.

"First, I have to get copies of all the phone numbers patched in to the Owens's house for the last two weeks. Then I'm putting Bryan on salary. We'll find him a cubicle at the office with a phone. He will call each computer owner he personally offended and schedule appointments to make an on-site visit to either repair the problems or take them a brand new computer which he will install free of charge.

"Secondly, he will answer their questions and give them help until they are satisfied that Dunbarton's is a company that can admit it makes mistakes, but is willing to rectify them.

"Thirdly, with his hourly wage he'll pay his uncle two weeks rent for the unauthorized use of his house.

"Last but not least, he will confess everything he's done to his parents and try to get back a level of trust."

"What if he refuses?"

"I'd hate to think Bryan is that far gone."

"So would I." More quietly she said, "He's very blessed that it was your company he picked to inflict his reign of mayhem. I hope that one day, when he's a little more grown up, he'll understand what a great thing you were willing to do for him."

"The credit goes to you, Annabelle. Your initial compassion for Bryan has influenced my thinking. Since I trust your judgment, we'll stay with this plan and see what happens. Trina's part in all this will never come up."

"Thank you," she said in a small voice. "What are you going to do about the Iversons?"

Rand started the car and they headed back toward the freeway. "Whether I fire Barrett Iverson or not depends on how his brother managed to get the password from him. As for Paul, he'll have to sell the motorbike and give the money back to Bryan. Since he probably won't get full value for it, he'll have to work to make up the deficit. Hopefully it will be a salutary lesson in the hazards of manipulation and bribery."

She reached for her cellular phone. "As you said earlier, they don't know the real criminal actions they've committed. I need to call Roman and report what's happened. It's possible Bryan could be home with his parents before the night is over."

Many things are possible. When everything is cleared up, I plan to spend all my nights with you for the rest of our lives.

"Hi, Diana. It's Annabelle again. Any sign of Roman? I haven't heard from him yet."

I need another case to work on. Tonight.

"That's because Roman's wife went into labor."

"You're kidding!" The news filled Annabelle with excitement for them, but it seemed she would have to find another solution to her problem. "Their first baby... Roman must be euphoric."

"If you want to know the truth, he's a complete and total wreck. When she called him to come home, he went deathly pale, then flew out of here like a shot. I would never have thought our boss could act like that. I'm afraid you're going to have to wait to talk to him. There's a long list ahead of you as it is."

"That's okay. When Roman eventually makes contact with you, give him and Brittany my best wishes and tell him the Ludlow case has been solved. Hopefully I'll have things wound up by tonight."

"You *found* Bryan Ludlow already?"

"Yes. Roman can reach me on the cellular for the details whenever he finds time to call. Talk to you later."

"I take it your boss is at the hospital with his wife," Rand murmured when she put the phone away.

"Yes. According to Diana, he's a nervous wreck."

Annabelle didn't understand when she felt Rand's hand reach out and cover hers. His fingers tightened enough that she couldn't pull away.

"Do you know, I'll probably be close to certifiable by the time my wife goes into labor for the first time."

So he *was* planning to get married one day... Just not to her. When a man as inexorably masculine as Rand admitted to that kind of fear, the last superficial barrier she'd erected against him crumbled. The pain went on and on. This time when she tried to remove her hand, he finally let it go.

"After losing your mother, it's no wonder your father guarded and cherished you so closely all of his life."

"He should have married again. I always wanted a mother."

"Some men can only love once."

Annabelle shook her head. "I don't believe that. He didn't try to look for anyone else."

"He obviously thought she was perfect and figured no one else could ever measure up." There was a brief pause. "He probably didn't think any boys were good enough for you, either."

She moved restlessly in her seat. "You're right. He didn't."

"What do you think he would have thought of me?"

The air seemed to leave her lungs. "Since there is no *us,* it's a moot point."

"Hypothetically speaking," he continued tenaciously.

"Hypothetically speaking he would have told me that a wealthy tycoon whose face appeared on the cover of *Today's Fortune* would want only one thing from a girl like me."

"Is that what *you* think?" Their tires screeched as he turned into the Dunbarton parking lot, then shut off the motor.

"Frankly, I haven't given it any thought. I'm the private detective assigned to your case."

"You're a hell of a lot more than that," he ground out savagely.

The next thing she knew, he'd pulled her across the seat into his arms. Rand was so much bigger and stronger than she was, there was no way to evade him or the mouth that descended on hers with stifling force.

"Rand—" She cried his name, unable to deny her need of him. Caught off guard, she had no will to resist and began giving him kiss for kiss, each one deeper and more sensuous than the last until her body trembled from desire.

When he unexpectedly tore his lips from hers, she was so far gone, she moaned in agony.

"Did you hear that?" he demanded with quiet ferocity, his lips moving against her throat. "You want this as much as I do. If you and I shared a simple business relationship, your heart wouldn't be running away with you. Your lovely body wouldn't fit into mine like it was made for me. Admit it, Annabelle."

"I've never denied it," she whispered shakily.

"Then don't tell me there's no *us.*' Suddenly he let her go. "Now that we have that settled, shall we join Howard and start to wrap up this case?"

Annabelle scrambled out her side of the car, embarrassed because it was after five o'clock and there were people in the parking lot who'd seen them kissing.

"Don't worry about our audience," he murmured in an aside. "They're just envious."

Rand had no idea how much his bantering wounded

her. She hurried on ahead, but in reality she was running away from a situation that was out of control.

She was out of control.

Later on tonight, when they'd had their talk with Bryan and had gone back to her house, she would tell Rand to gather up his things and move to the hotel. *Out of her life.*

Of course life as she knew it would never have the same meaning again. His coming to Salt Lake had ruined any hope she might have entertained that she could get over him. But lots of people still functioned, even with fatal diseases. Rand was her fatal disease. Somehow she would learn to survive.

It was almost one in the morning when Rand pulled the rental car into Annabelle's driveway. With the case solved, he had anticipated what was coming next, and had already prepared for that eventuality with a counterattack of his own.

He knew exactly what she was doing as she volunteered to make coffee for them. She was getting ready to deliver a quaint little speech and order him from her house, in the nicest way possible of course.

"I hope you're not doing this for me," he whispered near her ear. "Much as I would love it, I've got business to do and need my briefcase, so I'm going to head on back to the hotel. If you'll just give me a minute to get my things from downstairs, I'll be out of your hair."

Without waiting for a reaction, he disappeared down the steps to the basement study and turned on her computer. She'd sent a fax to Janet. He needed to know what it said.

He didn't care if what he was doing was criminal or immoral. Rand was fighting for his life.

When he looked in her fax file, he realized she'd deleted the message.

No matter. It would have been sent to the trash bin and he doubted she'd had time to delete that, too.

He hadn't realized he'd been holding his breath until he found the fax in question and recovered it.

Lord. The message turned out to be more revealing than he could ever have hoped for.

He read the next to the last line over again. *Which goes to show he never understood me, otherwise he would realize head of security is not the position I had in mind.*

His eyes closed tightly for a moment while he willed his heart to stop its thunderous pounding.

Tomorrow he would pay Janet a visit. Once she knew his intentions, he had no worry about her agreeing to help him. Roman had already been in on the plan from the beginning. The only person in the dark was Annabelle. This was one time when his undercover Venus wouldn't have a clue what hit her until it was too late.

"Annabelle? Thanks for coming in early."

"No problem, Roman. How are Brittany and little Yuri?"

Roman's white smile dazzled her. "They're both wonderful."

Annabelle's eyes closed tightly for a minute. *How*

would it feel to be that happy? To be married to the person you loved? To have his baby? "I'm so happy for you, Roman."

"I know that. Now, let's talk about you."

She hunched her shoulders. "There's nothing to talk about."

"I think there is. Since the Ludlow case was closed a month ago, you've not only taken on one new assignment after the other, you've been providing non-stop backup for the rest of the guys. At the rate you're going, you'll burn yourself out. I don't want to see that happen."

She swallowed hard. "I like to stay busy. Has someone complained about my work?"

"Annabelle—" He frowned. "You know better than that. All the PI's have been talking about the masterful job you did on finding Bryan Ludlow. Because of your expert handling of the situation, the police were kept out of it and there was no public scandal. Congratulations."

"Thank you, Roman, but the people you should really be praising are Trina and Rand. He's the one who chose not to prosecute the parties involved."

Roman sat back in his swivel chair, eyeing her narrowly. "I'm fully aware of the part both of them played in the case. Undoubtedly Rand's help brought it to a close that much sooner, but you were the one who listened to Trina in the first place and got that boy's voice on tape. One of the best things I ever did was hire you to come work for me."

She could feel the sincerity behind his words. "Thank you."

"You're welcome. You also need to know that Rand is manifestly grateful, as you can well imagine."

"Despite what all the guys are twittering about, I didn't sleep with him, Roman."

"I never thought you did."

"Even when the guys told you he stayed at my house?"

"No. I know you too well. You're exactly like Brittany. You weren't working for me when I went undercover as her husband during that stalking case. The guys razzed me about it constantly. But the fact is, I didn't go to bed with her until our wedding night."

"Well, I'm afraid Rand's and my undercover caper didn't end quite like yours."

"But you *are* in love with him."

Annabelle couldn't lie to Roman. "Unfortunately I am." Her voice trembled.

"And he's not in love with you?"

"No."

"How do you know?"

"Because the word 'marriage' never came up. On that same night—which was the night we tied up all the loose ends of the Ludlow case—he drove me home, gathered up his things, thanked me, said goodbye and left. I haven't seen or heard from him since."

"I'm sorry you've been in so much pain, Annabelle. Maybe what I have to tell you will be of some comfort. When he paid the bill, he asked me to give you this." Roman handed her a manila envelope. "Go ahead. Open it."

Her heart skipped a beat. "No. I'd better not."

"I believe it's your bonus. Something about a trip to the Mediterranean."

Rand remembered. Her hand shook as she put the packet back on Roman's desk. "I can't accept this."

"Why not? He thought the trouble in Salt Lake might take months to solve. Within a few days' time you caught the perpetrator and saved his company hundreds of thousands of dollars. The man can't thank you enough and wants you to enjoy this bonus. I agree with him that you deserve it."

She averted her eyes. "I—I can't do it. Please— will you return it for me?"

"You won't do it yourself?"

"I'd rather not."

"He warned me you might be difficult."

Annabelle felt heat creep up her neck into her face.

"I understand he offered you the job of head of security for his company."

Her head flew back. "He told you *that?*"

Roman's inscrutable expression revealed nothing about his thoughts. "Isn't it the truth?"

"Well, yes—but—"

"Apparently he said you could still work for me and do the security job, as well."

She fumbled with her Jeep keys. "I didn't think he really meant it."

"Do you want the job?"

"No!"

"That's pretty emphatic. Electronics are right up your alley. Heading security for Dunbarton's is the kind of position any top computer engineer in the country would kill for.''

"I don't want to leave Salt Lake."

"Not even for a few days out of every month?"

"No. I like the job I've got."

"Not even for a six digit figure salary?"

"I wouldn't know what to do with that much money."

He tapped a pencil against the desktop. "He warned me you would turn down the job and the salary, so he has asked me if I would allow you some time off to work at home on a new foolproof security system for his company.

"Only you and he would know what it is, making it virtually impossible for another hacker to be successful. He'll pay the agency price for your time. Would you be interested?''

"I don't need to stay home. I already have one worked out. I've been doing it in my spare time for years."

A long silence ensued. "So what are you saying? Can he buy it from you?"

"He can *have* it."

"Annabelle—you don't give something like that away. Any computer-run company in the world—including governmental agencies or NASA for example—would pay huge sums for such a system."

"That's true, but you don't know something I know."

"What's that?"

"While I was undercover, I kind of ruined things

between him and the woman he'd been seeing in Phoenix before he came here.''

"How could you do that?"

She heaved a deep sigh, then told him what had happened in Rand's hotel room. "So you see, I owe him.''

"But he told you she showed up uninvited, and he assured you he was never in love with her, so you haven't ruined anything.''

"Maybe. Maybe not.''

"What are you so scared of?"

Roman had just zeroed in on the problem. "Rand and I broke up in the first place because he doesn't want a wife who works. I happen to love my work, so nothing has changed between us. It's better if I don't see him again. When we're together—'' She couldn't finish what she was going to say.

Compassion shone from his eyes. "I get that same feeling around Brittany. It's called 'love.' When I finally recognized it for what it was, I had to do something about it.''

"Well, you were lucky because she was in love with you, too. My situation is vastly different.''

"So you wouldn't consider flying to Phoenix to help install this new security system for him?"

"No. I have everything on disks. Since he's been in touch with you, I'll package them up and give them to you to send to him. He's brilliant. He'll be able to install the system himself.''

"All right. Enough said about Rand. I've got a new case for you.''

Thank heaven. The mention of Rand was too painful a subject to even contemplate.

"Gladstone Realty has sold a house to a party from out of town. The painting and carpeting have been done along with the basic decorating. Apparently the purchaser wants the place rigged with security inside and out before they move in."

"Why did they come to us?"

"They don't trust a retail business operation. One of its employees might take advantage later on. If we install everything, it will be done by bonded experts without the neighbors being aware of it. You're our electronic wizard. I thought this job sounded tailor-made for you."

"What do they want included, exactly?"

"Everything. Bug detectors, telephone taps, surveillance equipment and audio cameras, alarms. They'd like the job finished three days from today. It ought to be a lot of fun."

"Are they diamond merchants or something?"

Roman smiled. "Maybe they're like a certain female PI I know, and just want to *feel* safe." That comment brought a reciprocal smile to her lips. Her first in a month. "You'll have to change all the locks. Price is no object."

"You shouldn't have told me that. I'll probably get carried away."

"Why do you think I picked you?" Roman winked. "When you've finished, I can guarantee the owner a fail-proof job. The only people who will ever touch foot on that property without anyone knowing about it will have to drop out of the sky. Even then, alarms will go off giving the invaders cardiac arrest before they ever land.''

"You think I'm that good?''

"According to Gerard, your place is better protected than Fort Knox.''

She couldn't meet his eyes. "You heard about that?''

"Annabelle— You know there aren't any secrets around here. I'll alert Brittany that you'll be over to the house sometime today to start loading up the equipment you'll need.''

"That's perfect. I can't wait to see little Yuri. I have a present for him.''

His gray eyes gleamed. "To show you my appreciation, you can rummage around my basement as long as you want. Big Yuri sent us a shipment of new gadgets. You should have a field day. What disguise shall I tell her you'll be using?''

"A Triple-A Bug Exterminators's truck. I can rent it and a uniform whenever I want.''

"Here's the envelope with the address and the keys. Everything's labeled. Good luck.''

As she reached the door, he called to her. She turned around. He was holding up the vacation packet Rand had sent. "You're sure you want this to go back to him?''

Her heart felt like it had been stabbed. "I'm positive.'' She hadn't seen Rand for a month. Maybe one day, if she lived long enough, she could wrench him from her consciousness.

"So be it.''

Within an hour Annabelle, dressed in a denim-blue

uniform resembling a jumpsuit, drove the extermina-
tor truck above the state capitol grounds to a wealthy
residential area. The spectacular view overlooked the
entire Salt Lake Valley.

If Annabelle had her choice, this spot which was a
thousand feet above the desert floor, would be the
place where she would build a house because she
could see the Great Salt Lake to the west, Mount
Nebo to the south, and the Wasatch mountains to the
east.

To live here with Rand would be all she asked of
life. *You're living in a fairy tale again, Annabelle.*

She dashed the tears from her eyes and kept driving
past one beautiful home after another. The houses at
the top—partially hidden from the street by foliage—
held the commanding view.

Annabelle searched for addresses painted on the
curb until she found the one she'd been looking for.
A soft gasp escaped when she lifted her gaze to the
charming French country home landscaped around a
stand of birch and ornamental topiary trees.

Like a *mas* lifted straight out of the lavender fields
of Provence, it was a little jewel of architecture and
could have been made for her. She couldn't wait to
see what the owners had done to the interior.

Her plan of action was to ascertain what she would
need to make everything secure before she ran by
Roman's to pick up all the new electronic devices.
But one step inside the house and she forgot her mission.

The four-bedroom home, partially furnished, was a
dream of pale yellow, cream and white, her favorite

colors. Dark wood beams on the walls and ceiling gave the authentic look of a small Mediterranean villa.

Beyond the adorable kitchen with its tiled fireplace and French doors lay a terrace all in tile with an herb garden. Grass ran to the edge of the rim. No trees encumbered the spectacular view. To Annabelle, the place was pure enchantment.

A new ache settled around the region of her heart as she imagined inhabiting this paradise with the man she loved above all else, filling it with happiness and love. Filling it with their children.

When she realized how far her thoughts had wandered, she gave herself a severe talking to, then got to work taking notes of all the things she would need. A half hour later she reluctantly let herself out again to drive to Roman's.

What might have taken three days to accomplish ended up taking only two because Annabelle had fallen in love with the home and never wanted to be away from it. Horrified that she'd shortchanged herself a day of pure bliss, she couldn't bring herself to report that the job was finished until the end of the third day.

Of course she would only charge for two days' labor. If she were being truly honest, she ought to pay the owner for loitering on the premises the third day just to drink in its beauty.

Toward dinnertime, she started to feel guilty and decided it was time to leave. As she was gathering up her tools a high-pitched, reverberating siren went off, causing her to jump. Someone was approaching the house. She'd covered it from every angle.

The sirens could be shut off or turned on manually from a control panel she'd placed in the hall wall next to the walk-in pantry. If the owners went on vacation, they could switch everything to automatic which would alert the police who would reset the mechanisms.

Annabelle dashed to the hall to see which light had gone on and discovered that someone had come up the front walkway. She turned on the monitor to pick up the visual from the hidden camera. It revealed a man at the front door. But his dark head was turned as if he were looking at the street, so she couldn't see his face. So far everything was working perfectly.

She'd been in contact with Gladstone Realty and assumed he was the Realtor they'd sent to inspect the job before they asked her to sign the job completion form. Confident that he wouldn't be disappointed, she turned off the siren, then hurried through the house and unlocked the door.

Still halfway turned, the man with the black wavy hair looked increasingly familiar. The double-breasted gray tickweave suit and white shirt with a tie in a small geometric design couldn't disguise his big, masculine physique. It was very much like... But it couldn't be.

Then he turned his head.

"*Rand!*" she gasped out loud.

"Annabelle."

Once again she felt the world spin.

He didn't say anything, but those flame blue eyes studied her burnished curls and facial features minus any makeup for an overly long moment.

Slowly his intimate gaze swept down her body still encased in the ghastly uniform and she could have died of embarrassment.

"W-what are you doing here?" she demanded in a tone that sounded too sharp, even to her ears. But she couldn't help it. How could he have done this to her?

There'd been no warning, no chance to make herself presentable. He, on the other hand, stood there with one hand in his pocket, looking sophisticated and indolently at ease. It wasn't fair.

"I had to come to Salt Lake on business," he said in a mild voice. "Roman said I would find you here."

She could hardly swallow. "I thought you were the Realtor."

His shuttered eyes gave him a vaguely brooding look. "Your latest conquest?"

"What?"

"When Roman told me you not only turned down the head of security position in the company I offered you, but you refused the bonus that was promised, I assumed it was because you had a male interest that prevented you from wanting to leave Salt Lake, even for two short weeks. Did you patch things up with Gerard? That was his name, wasn't it?"

Gerard? How did he remember that?

"Don't be absurd."

His expression hardened. "I've been accused of many things, but no one ever attributed that particular word to me before."

"I didn't mean to sound rude," she answered, trying desperately to maintain her poise when she was on the verge of hysteria. "Gerard is a colleague and friend, nothing more."

"Good. Shall we start again? Why don't you ask me how I am."

She bit her lip. "It's obvious you're fine. How's Caroline?"

His smile didn't reach his eyes which at the moment had a slightly glacial aspect. "The last thing I heard, she was in Europe. Aren't you going to invite me in?"

Nervousness had forced her to rub her palms against her hips. "I can't. The Realtor— Oh! There he is!"

A station wagon with the words Gladstone Realty pulled into the driveway next to her truck. She noticed that Rand's rental car had been parked against the curb.

The man, mid-forties, got out of his car and walked toward them with an oversize smile on his face. "Hi! I'm Bruce Varney. I came to see how your work is progressing. I thought you should know that the owner will be returning later this evening."

"Hello, Mr. Varney," Rand interjected before Annabelle could open her mouth to speak. He stepped forward and both men shook hands. "I'm Ray, Annabelle's husband."

Annabelle couldn't believe Rand's nerve, but she didn't dare gainsay him in front of the Realtor.

"Pleased to meet you. Are you with the Lufka agency, too?"

"That's right. We work together on most cases, don't we, darling."

"That's true," she grumbled under her breath. "Come in, Mr. Varney. Everything's done. I'll go through the house with you while you make your inspection. If you're satisfied, then I'll sign the paperwork."

"Since you're about through, I'll go on home and meet you there, sweetheart," Rand piped up congenially. "After you have a nice soak in the tub, we'll enjoy dinner someplace special."

Dinner?

Annabelle almost stumbled over her tool case. She didn't know what game he was playing, yet under the circumstances it seemed easier to go along with him.

"Whatever you say, *darling.*"

"I promise this inspection won't be a lengthy one," Mr. Varney assured them.

With the other man looking on in avid interest, Rand pulled her close and brushed his lips against her cheek. "I can't wait till we're alone."

Rand smelled so good and familiar wearing that woodsy-scented aftershave she loved.

Like setting a lighted match to dry tinder, the feel of his possessive mouth against her skin sent fire spiraling to every cell of her inflamed body. Over the past month she'd tried to suppress the yearning for his touch. Now her hunger for him had been stirred up all over again, leaving her with an ache that would never go away.

In a daze, she watched him leave before she turned her attention back to the Realtor. Ten minutes later he pronounced that she'd done a perfect job. Pleased, she signed the work order, said goodbye to him and drove to Triple-A Bug Exterminators to return the truck and equipment before going home.

Throughout the entire drive, her heart beat a fierce tattoo in anticipation of being with Rand later in the evening.

He said he'd come back to Salt Lake on business. Why had he sought her out? What did he want?

Even though the answers didn't matter because in the long run she would never be that important to him, she still felt at a total disadvantage.

How could he do this to her? How could he just appear out of nowhere and start kissing her, touching her, when she knew it meant so little to him?

The best thing to do was wait until he arrived at the house, then tell him through the door that it had been nice to see him again but she wasn't interested in catching up on old news and had other plans. That ought to put him off for good.

Right now she was fighting a battle of survival. Didn't he know that he was her whole life, that she couldn't handle seeing him every once in a while only to go through another devastating separation?

CHAPTER NINE

RAND reached her house before she did and parked his rental car around the corner so Annabelle wouldn't know he was already ensconced. He'd purposely rigged the alarm so it would stay on even if she tried to deactivate it. That way he would know when she was coming up the back steps.

Having discarded his suit coat and rolled up his shirt sleeves, he went to work putting together the Italian dinner he'd been preparing since morning. All he had left to do was make the green salad. He'd already set the table in the dining room with fresh flowers and wine. Everything stood in readiness.

As he was adding the pesto sauce to the pasta, the siren sounded. That set his adrenaline surging. The next thing he knew, he heard a key in the lock and the back door opened. He pretended that he didn't know she was standing there in shock while he finished adding some balsamic vinegar to the olive oil.

Finally the siren shut off. After the din, the silence seemed even more pronounced.

"Who gave you permission to enter my house uninvited?"

Carrying the salad to the dining room he said over his shoulder, "I didn't think I needed it. Since you refused the vacation packet and turned down my job offer, I decided the only way to properly thank you

157

for your invaluable help in tracking down Bryan Ludlow was to fix you dinner.''

He fought to repress a smile because she had followed him into the other room where more silence ensued.

''I know how tired you are after being on a case and thought you might like a nice quiet meal at home. Since I forgot to return the spare key before I left for Phoenix, I thought this might be a nice way to give it back, along with my sincerest thanks for everything. I promise to do the dishes when we're through eating,'' he added.

Rand could feel her struggle and held his breath. She had every right to throw him out. It had taken a month to accomplish everything he had to do. In that time he hoped she'd gone crazy without him. Not seeing or talking to her for thirty days had been the worst deprivation of his life.

''I—I have to shower first.''

''Take your time,'' he said softly, afraid to look at her for fear she would see the light in his eyes. The time away from her had proved to him that he couldn't exist without her.

To get his mind off of her standing beneath the spray, all warm and vulnerable, he went into the living room to read the newspaper. But certain intimate pictures continued to haunt his consciousness until he eventually set down the paper in disgust and got up to pace.

That's when she walked in the living room, her freshly washed curls bouncing. A subtle peach fragrance emanated from her while he stood there stunned by her appearance.

Instead of one of her disguises, or her usual T-shirt and jeans, she was wearing a tailored white silk blouse with French cuffs and palazzo pants in a tiny black on white print, revealing the breathtaking form of her voluptuous body beneath the filmy material.

Black Italian sandals with heels added several inches to her height. Gypsy-styled earrings glinted silver in the light with every heartbeat. Annabelle Forrester was a raving beauty. He had to use the greatest self-control not to crush her in his arms.

"You look lovely," he whispered huskily.

"Thank you. I'm going to the ballet later tonight with Janet, so I thought it would be wise to get ready now."

She was a wonderful liar. He happened to know Janet was finishing up final plans for *him*.

"While I was downtown earlier, I saw that *Odile* is playing at the opera house. Do you go often?"

"Whenever I can."

"Since you have a big night ahead of you, then we don't have much time to enjoy our dinner. Shall we eat?"

A little pulse throbbed madly at the base of her throat. There was a slight tremor of her hands as she adjusted an earring. He rejoiced that she was on the verge of losing control.

Sexual attraction wasn't something a person could hide, though she was trying valiantly not to let it show. *You want me as much as I want you, Annabelle.*

You love me. The vibes were so strong, they were almost tangible.

He followed her to the dining room and helped her to the table. She would never know the moral fortitude it took to remove his hand from her elbow when he wanted to explore every inch of her face and body.

"How is Bryan Ludlow these days? Did he repair all the damage?" she asked after he'd brought the food from the kitchen and they'd started to eat.

Her nearness made concentration almost impossible. "Yes. In fact he worked harder at making amends than I would have guessed. Because of his new attitude and appreciation for his parents, he now has a permanent job with us."

She swallowed a little of the wine he'd poured. "That's quite a turnaround for him and kind of you. Did you ever find out where the barking dog came from?"

"As a matter of fact I did." Rand smiled. "It belonged to the neighbor family down the street who had originally been asked to look after the mail and water the plants while the Owens were gone. Apparently Bryan worked out an arrangement with them and even offered to watch their dog. Sometimes Paul went over to help tend it with him."

"Partners in crime," she murmured. "I'm glad Barrett Iverson wasn't implicated."

"So am I. Paul made a clean confession. He watched his brother when he worked on the computer at home and discovered the password on his own. After what happened, I doubt he'll do anything like that again."

"Let's hope not." She wiped the corner of her mouth with a napkin.

There was a tension-filled pause. He wondered what was coming next. "Rand— Have you been in touch with Roman since you came to town?"

"As a matter of fact I have. He tried to give me the disks you left him, but I told him to give them back to you."

Her eyes widened. "Why? Have you found a better security system?"

"No, but since you're the creator, you're the only person who should install it. Roman told me you weren't interested in coming to Phoenix for any reason, so I couldn't accept your gift."

"But—"

"Did I misunderstand him, Annabelle?" he inquired with deceiving mildness. "Or have you changed your mind?"

She was looking down at her plate where she'd barely made inroads on her food. Apparently her appetite had deserted her, another good sign that his unexpected appearance had thrown her off balance.

"No. My life is here in Salt Lake." Her voice shook.

"It's a great place to live. You have the four seasons, the mountains and a career you love. What more do you need?" he baited her, impatient for her surrender.

She suddenly pushed herself away from the table and stood up.

"Thank you for the delicious meal, Rand."

"You're entirely welcome."

"I'm sorry I can't eat the rest, but it's g-getting late," she stammered. "I'm going to have to leave here in a minute."

"I'll do the dishes and clean up. Annabelle—would you mind if I stayed here for a little while before I call for a taxi? To be truthful, I'm tired. Maybe its the change in altitude, but I'm suddenly craving sleep."

She darted him what he hoped was an anxious glance. "I thought you looked a little less rested than usual."

So she had noticed.

He raked a hand through his hair. "I guess I've been working too many hours since we last saw each other and it has finally caught up with me. If I could just lie down on your living room couch for an hour, then I'll be on my way."

Her intense gaze seemed to be looking for something elusive. "Whenever my father felt ill, he would say he was tired because he didn't want me to worry. I have a feeling you're hiding something more serious from me. If you're sick, then you should be in bed."

"I'm not sure what I am, but I don't want to take advantage."

"Don't be ridiculous. You can sleep in Dad's room. It's only a double bed because he wasn't a big man. I'm afraid I don't have any pajamas that would fit."

"It doesn't matter. Right now, any bed sounds divine."

"Come with me."

Forced once more to tamp down his delight, he followed her beautiful body through the house, not feeling the slightest degree of guilt over the turn of events he had purposely orchestrated.

His plan to arouse her compassion had proved successful. Would her concern for his welfare extend to staying home and not going out after all?

Rand knew she'd made up the business about the ballet on the spur of the moment so she wouldn't have to deal with him.

I have news for you, my love.

Rand stripped down to his boxers, then got in bed and closed his eyes.

Annabelle tapped on the door minutes later. "If there's anything you need, just call out."

He pretended to be asleep. Soon enough he would know if she was too anxious about him to leave the house.

"*Rand?*" came a whisper.

She sounded worried. Still he ignored her.

The bedroom had two windows facing the driveway. If she were to go anywhere in her Jeep, he would hear the motor.

For a long time he listened, but there was no sound. She'd opted to stay home with him.

Just knowing they were under the same roof brought him a sense of peace which had been missing for the past month. When he'd first suggested that she work out of the hotel while he stayed at her house, he'd purposely offered to sleep in her basement because he hadn't wanted to seem presumptuous. He hadn't dared make a mistake.

But things were different now.

He turned over on his stomach and buried his face in the pillow, imagining her in the bed with him.

Soon the real thing would replace his dreams.

To his shock, Rand came awake much later in a room filled with sunlight. He sat straight up, glancing at the bedside clock. It was 10:20 a.m.

He bit out an epithet. The plan had been to stay in bed an hour, then get up for a drink and run into Annabelle, showing surprise that she hadn't gone to the ballet after all. They would talk a little until he'd broken her down enough to start making love to her. Then he would ask her to marry him.

That was almost twelve hours ago. He'd been so emotionally exhausted from their separation, the relief at being united again had made him pass out cold.

But he was wide awake now. What an irony when he knew she could still be asleep in the next room. Much as he would love to climb under her covers and kiss her awake, he couldn't do that.

A cold shower was in order.

He jackknifed out of bed and slipped on his suit trousers, then headed for the bathroom at the other end of the hall.

"Rand?"

He turned around, barely able to distinguish her silhouette in the semidarkness of the hall.

"Are you still sick?"

"Not at all," he assured her. "The sleep did me wonders. I was just going to get some water."

"I made you some iced tea with lemons and oranges. Dad said it always helped settle a sick stomach. Would you like a glass now?"

"I'd love it."

"Come in the kitchen then."

"I can get it. You go ahead and do whatever you need to do."

"I've been awake for hours reading and could use some, too."

She had stayed up through the night watching over him.

About now his guilt kicked in, but he kept telling himself that all was fair in love and war. The situation with Annabelle constituted both.

His gaze sought her out as she opened the refrigerator. If she'd thought that her night apparel camouflaged her exceptional feminine attributes, she was mistaken.

The hunter green, long-sleeved, knee-length robe cinched at the waist by the belt revealed the womanly shape beneath, exposing her shapely bare legs for his perusal.

He didn't look away when she shut the refrigerator door and turned around. Her attractively disheveled curls glistened like rich chestnuts in the light. The eyes beneath the dark fringe of her lashes gave off a golden glow.

Heat filled her cheeks before she hurriedly looked away from his shoulders and chest with its mat of black hair. He had a feeling she liked what she saw. But he knew this kind of intimacy was foreign to her. Her modesty and virtue were just some of the traits he loved about her.

"How was the ballet?" he asked after she'd handed

him a glass. They both stood against the counter facing each other.

She took a long swallow of her drink before answering. "I-it was wonderful."

You still can't admit what you're feeling, but I'm making headway because you didn't throw me out last night.

"*Odile* is one of the darker love stories I believe. Mind if I take a look at the program?"

"I'm afraid I got there a little too late to get one. How does the iced tea taste to you?"

"It's delicious." He meant it. "You've added mint."

She nodded. "I keep fresh leaves on hand."

"I could get addicted to this. Is there any more?"

"Of course." She reached for the pitcher in the fridge and topped his glass again. "You seem to be feeling much better."

"I am. Forgive me for crashing on you like that."

Their eyes held. "Obviously you needed the sleep. If you'd like to take a shower, go ahead. I've put fresh towels on the rack and there's a new toothbrush on the sink."

He drained his glass in one go. "Thank you. I think I'll take you up on your offer."

Today of all days he needed to feel and look his best.

"I was going to say that after my shower I'd clean up the mess I made in here last night, but I can see you've already done it."

"After the marvelous dinner you cooked, it was the

least I could do." Her hands plunged into her robe pockets. "Rand—are you really all right?"

"If I weren't, you would know about it. Believe me. I'm ready to tackle the world today."

His comment brought the first hint of a smile to her enchanting face. That picture accompanied him to the shower.

As he stood beneath the spray, the ramifications of the lie he'd told last night sobered him when he realized how much trust she'd placed in him. Annabelle wasn't the kind of woman to let just any man invade her space like this. It touched him deeply that she'd left out her father's electric shaver for his use. As far as Rand was concerned, this was the moment he'd been waiting for...

Annabelle's heart was in her throat as she prepared eggs and toast for both of them. She had this premonition he was going to leave this morning and she'd never see him again.

Whatever had caused him to collapse like that last night had brought home the fact that he was her life, her entire world! Too many times last night she'd peeked in his room to see if he was all right. Each time she went in, she lingered a little longer. The wicked part of her had hoped he would be too ill to get up this morning. Then she could insist that he stay in bed all day while she pampered him.

Her fantasies had gone so far as to imagine him begging her to lie down next to him and somehow they would get in each other's arms and he would tell her he couldn't live without her.

I want to be his wife.

She smothered a little sob and dashed in her bedroom to get dressed. Her father's words played over and over in her mind. "When you meet the right one, you'll just know. It'll seem natural and right."

Annabelle *did* know. Everything seemed perfectly natural and perfectly right.

But if I'm the only one who feels this way....

With trembling hands she pulled a new silky pantsuit in a café-au-lait color from the closet. Toned with a blouse in an eggshell hue, it looked feminine and smart.

If this was the last time they would ever be together, she wanted him to leave with the best memory of her.

As she slipped into another pair of dark-brown sandals with wedges, a picture of Caroline dressed in some heavenly peach creation tore at her self-confidence. Annabelle could never look like the kind of woman Rand normally associated with. He needed someone tall and willowy. Just remembering what he looked like without a shirt reduced her limbs to water.

Not only was he a gorgeous male, he was a brilliant, sophisticated man so far beyond her reach, she wondered at her temerity in even entertaining dreams about him.

You're such a little fool, Annabelle. A few stolen kisses doesn't constitute undying love or anything close to it. Rand wants a stay-at-home wife. Whatever made you think he had changed his mind?

A few minutes later Rand met her in the kitchen. By tacit agreement they stood around to eat the way a married couple might do who were comfortable with each other.

Her pain intensified because she knew he was on the verge of leaving. "More eggs?"

The desire for food had left her. She couldn't even finish a piece of toast. Rand, on the other hand, appeared to have a healthy appetite and finished hers off as well the rest of the iced tea.

"I feel like a new man this morning," he announced after putting his dishes in the sink. "It's all because of you, Annabelle," he said with his back to her. "Now I'll get out of your hair and call for a taxi."

Her heart thudded sickeningly. "There's no need for that. I—I'll drive you back to your hotel. I'm leaving here anyway to run by the office. Roman will be assigning me a new case this morning and I have a ton of paperwork to do before our meeting. Shall we go?" *That was coming back to earth with a vengeance.*

As they started out the door, Rand reached for the key he'd left on the counter and handed it to her. "I promise I didn't have another one made, so you don't need to fear that I'll break in again, unannounced."

Another mortal wound. "I wasn't worried," she managed to say in a level tone though it was killing her, and put it in her purse.

"If the rest of the world were half as trusting as you," he murmured on their way out.

Annabelle almost missed a step because his comment was so ludicrous. She was probably the most paranoid person she knew, but Rand had changed her world for all time. He'd taken her heart by storm. By last night's actions, she'd practically told him she was his for the taking.

He's not interested, Annabelle, and you're never going to recover.

Once he'd helped her into the Jeep and had gone around to the passenger side, she turned on the ignition and backed out of the driveway.

Rand chuckled.

"What's so funny?" she demanded as they drove down the street to circle around and eventually enter the freeway headed north.

"You drive this thing like your motorcycle. I've decided you should have been a Formula I race car driver."

"Maybe you should have taken a taxi after all."

"I meant it as a compliment, Annabelle," he inserted suavely.

"Your talent behind the wheel shows the expertise of a professional driver."

Her nails dug into her palms around the steering wheel. The more she could feel him slipping away from her, the touchier she was growing.

The morning commute was over, but the traffic was still awful, adding frustration to unbearable pain.

"This city is impossible to navigate with all the construction going on. I'm going to get off at the next exit and drive in on Fifth East. In the long run it will be quicker."

"I'm in no hurry."

Dear God. I feel like it's the end of my life.

She turned on the radio to a talk-radio show and

left it there because she needed noise, anything to distract her until she was alone and could give way to her agony.

To her surprise, he turned it off after they'd gone a couple of blocks. "When you reach State Street, turn right and follow it all the way up."

Annabelle's delicately arched brows formed a frown. "What do you mean? Your hotel is on Sixth South and Main."

"I'm not staying at the Temple View this trip."

She took a fortifying breath. "I'm sorry. I just assumed."

"I notice you do a lot of that," he murmured.

Embarrassed because what he'd said was the truth she asked, "Then where are you staying?"

"It's no secret that I dislike living out of a dismal hotel room, so I made other arrangements."

She lurched forward. *Whose house would that be?*

Did he have a girlfriend here in Salt Lake? If he'd needed a ride, surely the other woman could have provided him transportation!

An attack of jealousy seized her until she almost lost control of the Jeep. "Where exactly does she live?"

"She?"

Scorching heat filled her cheeks. "The person you're staying with."

"I'm not staying with anyone. In fact I'm quite alone. Keep following State Street to the capitol, then wind up behind it."

When they came to a red light she practically stood on her brakes. "You mean the house you're staying at is in the same area where I was working yesterday?"

"That's right. I hope you don't mind. If I'm going to make you late for work, you can let me out at the capitol and I'll walk the rest of the way."

"As if I would do such a thing!" she snapped. Did he honestly believe she was *that* inconsiderate? Didn't he know better after the way she'd opened up her home and her heart to him last night?

By the time they drove past the prominent city landmark and proceeded up the steep hill behind it, she was consumed by curiosity.

"Are you renting?"

"No. I've bought myself a home."

What?

A rush of adrenaline quickened her body. "Why would you do that when you're hardly ever in Salt Lake?"

"That may have been true once, but certain things have changed. From now on, I'll be spending the bulk of my time here."

CHAPTER TEN

SUDDENLY Annabelle could hardly breathe. "How can you run your megacorporation from here when your headquarters are in Phoenix?"

"I've spent the last month training the new CEO for the company. As of two days ago, I stepped down and am only going to be involved at Dunbarton's in an advisory capacity."

Annabelle couldn't take it in. She'd thought that after this morning, he would be out of her life for good. It was easier that way. But to know he would be living in the same city, yet still out of reach, would *crucify* her.

"Your reaction is very reassuring," he murmured in a dry tone.

"I—I'm sorry. It's just that I can't imagine why you would want to move here when you've lived all your life in Phoenix."

"There was a time when I couldn't have imagined it, either, but life has a way of changing one's perspective. When I was in Salt Lake last month, I discovered that I not only liked it here, but I found a whole new career to interest me."

"*What* new career?" She could hardly talk because she had these suffocating bands constricting her chest.

"Oddly enough it's the same career you love."

It was a good thing they'd come to another light

because Annabelle would have slammed on the brakes anyway. "*You* want to be a PI?"

"That's right. After collaborating with you on the Ludlow case, I came to realize why you find this kind of work so fascinating. I don't think I've ever enjoyed anything as much in my life."

Annabelle had felt exactly the same way working with him. She couldn't believe what she was hearing.

"You were right to break off our engagement. I was a fool to expect you to give up a career you were made for, sweetheart."

Dear God.

"Those few days last month when you allowed me to tag along with you were a revelation. I was sorry you solved the case so fast. I wanted the experience to go on and on. So I asked Roman if he would consider hiring me on a probationary basis while I learn the business."

Cars from behind were honking at her because the light had turned green, but she sat there stupefied.

"It's going to take a long time, and I won't ever have the law enforcement and Interpol expertise that people like you and Gerard have brought to the agency, but I can provide backup and do behind-the-scenes work."

"And what did Roman say?" she finally asked in a tremulous voice.

"He was all for it, as long as *you* approved. He said his loyalty and allegiance were to you first, that if you felt uncomfortable with it, then he couldn't in good conscience welcome me aboard."

She thought she'd known real pain before now, but

she was wrong. Flooring the accelerator, the Jeep leaped ahead.

"Where do I go next?"

"Turn left at the top."

The *top?* But that was the street where she'd been working for the last three days!

"Actually, the answer is simple." He kept talking as if everything was perfectly normal. "All I'm asking you to do is think about it. You have to understand that coming to Salt Lake, working with you, made me reflect on my life and readjust my priorities. I've decided life's too short to go on being an empire builder."

"But you could still stay in Phoenix and be a PI there," she argued, fighting for her life. *I can't be in the same city with you, let alone work at the same job with you, Rand.*

"That's true, however I have another interest here in Salt Lake that outweighs all other considerations."

There *was* another woman.

The revelations dropping so hard and fast had knocked the pinnings out from under her. Tears blurred her eyes as she started down the street which was lined with cars on both sides.

"Turn left in the next driveway."

When she did his bidding, it took her a full minute to realize she was looking at the French country house she'd been working on over the past few days. Only today, there were hurricane lanterns tied with white ribbons lining the walkway that hadn't been there yesterday. It looked like someone was having a wedding.

She let out a muffled cry.

"What do you think of my home?"

She buried her face in her hands. *What do I think of the most wonderful, adorable house I've ever seen in my life? The one I've imagined living in with you?*

Annabelle couldn't take much more. She lifted her head again. "It's very nice." She didn't dare look at him. "Who's getting married?"

"*I* am."

She felt like she had just died. "Congratulations."

"Thank you. Won't you come in? Before the ceremony begins, my bride-to-be will want to thank you for making the house burglar-proof. She's the kind of woman who needs to feel safe in her own home."

Her hand practically broke the steering wheel in two. "I—I doubt very much your bride will be thinking about anything but getting married. Maybe another time. I—I'm late for my meeting with Roman."

"As a matter of fact, Roman's here to witness my nuptials. Come on inside. It will save you a trip to the office. He confided that he has a new case we can both work on after I get back from my honeymoon. That is, if you decide you don't mind my coming to work for the Lufka ag—"

"*Annie?*" a familiar female voice cried out, breaking in on their conversation.

Annabelle's head whipped around abruptly as the door on her side of the Jeep opened. "*Janet?* What are you doing here?" Her friend was all dressed up for the wedding. Annabelle felt like she was in the middle of a bad dream.

"What do you think? Rand invited me to watch him get married. Come on. Everyone's seated around back on the terrace waiting for the ceremony to begin. As for you, Rand, your nervous bride is terrified you weren't going to show up.''

Rand's bride had to be the woman Caroline had been talking about when she'd made that phone call to him in the hotel room.

"She still has a lot to learn about me," he murmured cryptically before levering himself from his side of the car. "See you two in a minute," came his parting remark before Annabelle watched his breathtaking male physique disappear around the side of the house in a few swift strides.

Janet pulled Annabelle's limp body from the Jeep. *Be strong, Annie. Don't let him know how this is affecting you.*

"I can't go in there!" she cried out in anguish.

"Oh, yes, you can. You have to! A year ago you walked away from him, and he let you go without looking back. Don't you see? *This* is your opportunity to show him what you're really made of, that the past is in the past. Where's your Forrester pride?

"If your dad were here, he'd tell you it's the right thing to do. It's kind of like seeing the body to believe the person is really dead. Watching Rand seal his doom will accomplish the same thing. It will end all your pain once and for all. I promise. In fact if you'll find a Bible, I'll swear an oath on it.''

Janet was her best friend. She was always right, about everything...

Seeing Rand get married would eventually have to put an end to the agony, wouldn't it?

"A-all right. I'll d-do it. But under no circumstances will I allow him to work for Roman after the honeymoon!''

"Good girl. Now you're talking! Let's go inside and freshen up before the ceremony starts. Gerard's saving seats on the patio.''

Gerard was here, too? Another pain pierced her heart. Rand certainly hadn't wasted any time getting chummy with the guys.

They headed for the front door. As soon as they reached the porch, an alarm sounded. Janet grinned. "You do good work, Annie.''

"It's Rand's fault if sirens go off during the ceremony,'' she bit out, still in shock and grief-stricken.

They entered through the front door and followed the hallway to the right wing of the house. Annie's steps faltered. "This is the way to the master bedroom.''

"I know. That's the room the guests are supposed to use.''

"But surely Rand is using his bedroom to get ready.''

"Not according to Diana who has been orchestrating everything.''

Diana had been planning his wedding for him?

Annabelle couldn't grasp what was happening. Between the state of her emotions and the continued blare of the alarm, she didn't know how she could move another step.

"Here we are.''

Janet opened the door as the alarm shut off. There stood Rand in a groom's black tux. He'd never looked so handsome. She couldn't bear it.

His searching gaze swerved to Annabelle. "Just in time to help me with this tie. Thanks for your help, Janet."

In the next breath he pulled Annabelle inside the room and shut the door. *They were alone.*

She twisted out of his arms, her breath coming in short pants. "What's going on, Rand?"

His mocking smile infuriated her. "A wedding."

"What is this?" she lashed out icily. "Did you decide to have a last-minute bachelor fling? Live it up with the old before you put on the new?"

His eyes glittered dangerously. "That's exactly what I had in mind."

"Stop it, Rand!"

"What is it, sweetheart?"

"Don't!" she blurted. "You're scaring me."

"Now you'll understand the state I've been in since we first met."

Her eyes rounded. "How could I scare you?"

"Far too easily. For once it's nice to have you at a disadvantage."

The next thing she knew, he'd picked her up and carried her to the king-size bed. When he followed her down, she was practically crushed by his huge body.

"Let's talk about *us*," he whispered against her lips.

"Please don't do this," she begged, her heart lurching crazily.

"Why not?"

"Because it's wrong!"

"How do you figure?" he murmured against her

throat, sending a yielding feeling of delight through her body.

"You're getting married in a few minutes." She half sobbed the words, trying to evade his mouth.

"That's right."

"Then why aren't you with your beloved?"

"Because you're in my blood and I can't seem to get you out."

"Does your fiancée know about this?"

"She does now."

"You can't do this to her!"

"Do what?" He devoured her mouth once more.

Her head thrashed about, forcing him to release her lips. "You know what I mean, Rand Dunbarton."

"I'm afraid I don't. You're going to have to spell it out for me."

"I can't when you're this close to me. I'm suffocating."

"You're exaggerating, sweetheart. We're having an intimate conversation. Nothing more."

"You're so big, you don't realize your own strength." She struggled for a little air. "I don't think very well on my back."

"I'm going to remember that," he vowed before his head descended and his mouth closed over hers, silencing her feeble protests with a kiss that literally consumed her.

There were degrees of kissing. He seemed to be giving her the kinds of kisses you gave the person you loved because you couldn't help yourself. It was impossible *not* to respond to his passion, but she

couldn't forget his bride-to-be was out there somewhere waiting...

Finally she managed to wrench her mouth from his.
"I'm just a plaything to you, like Caroline. Your poor
wife!"

His fingers tightened in her curls. The look of re-
fined savagery in his eyes sent a shiver through her
body. All hint of playfulness had vanished.

"I would never have spent the last month rearrang-
ing my business and my home, let alone my life, for
Caroline or any other female. There's only one
woman who has that kind of power over me and I'm
holding her in my arms."

It took Annabelle a minute to comprehend what he
was saying. "But you don't love me." Her voice
wobbled pitifully.

"I don't?"

The pointed question confused her. She was afraid
to believe what she was hearing. Searching his eyes
for the truth she cried softly, "You never said the
words."

A groan came out of him. "I thought I'd been
showing you how I felt ever since we met."

"Please don't tease me, Rand. I couldn't take it."

His eyes darkened. "Then that makes two of us."

"What do you mean?"

"I thought I was making myself perfectly clear. But
judging by your reaction, I'm beginning to think
maybe I was wrong about you. That you don't love
me as intensely as I love you."

"Not love you?" Tears stung her amber eyes.
"How can you say that when I'm so madly in love

with you, my world has no meaning without you! Why do you think I let you stay at my house last night, and those other nights, if you weren't the whole meaning of my existence?''

She couldn't stop the love pouring out of her. "After you left Salt Lake, I wanted to die. I adore you, Rand. I adore you," she murmured feverishly against his lips, wanting to climb right into his heart.

In the next breath he captured her mouth with his own. For a little while there was no reality but the rapture of being together, of touching and feeling and loving.

Engulfed in his powerful arms, Annabelle still couldn't get close enough. The freedom to love him totally acted like an aphrodisiac. Long-suppressed needs drove her to mold herself to him.

"If you left me now, I *would* die, Rand."

"*Thank God.*"

It seemed like Rand had been dreaming of this moment forever.

Annabelle's breathtaking response had already changed him into a different man, but he was fast losing control. This incredible woman had no comprehension of what she was doing to him.

"*Rand?*" she cried in protest when he lifted his mouth and removed her arms from around his neck.

Once on his feet, away from her sensuous warmth, he could think. "I'm sorry, sweetheart, but I intend to marry you before we enjoy our honeymoon."

"*Honeymoon?*" Her voice came out more like a squeak. It was the same happy sound he'd heard once before.

"If you'd taken the trouble to look inside that vacation packet I left with Roman, you would have realized there were tickets for Mr. and Mrs. Rand Dunbarton. We leave for Spain in the morning, which gives us just enough time to say our vows and get packed."

Suddenly she was on her dainty feet in the middle of his king-size bed, curls flopping, her eyes shimmering pure amber-gold. His own voluptuous little genie whose shoes had fallen off when their legs had become entwined.

"You really want to marry me?"

"I put this house in your name, Annabelle. You like it, don't you?"

"It's the most beautiful house—" Emotion robbed her of speech. He held out his arms and she came running across the top of the mattress.

At last.

He swung her around. "Does this mean you'll be my wife?"

She clung to him, nodding joyously. "I want to be everything to you. I want to fill this house with love. For the last three days, all I've done is imagine us here together. I want to make you *so* happy."

He finally put her down, cupping her adorable face in his hands. "You already have. It happened when you arrived with the bomb squad."

"I knew I was in love with you by the time you walked me out to the police car," she confessed breathlessly.

"Forgive me for being so arrogant, so full of pride? I wanted you all to myself and wasn't willing to share you with anything or anyone. But I know much better now. I've had a whole year to repent of my sins. Please tell me you'll give me another chance," he begged. "I'm a changed man, sweetheart. I'll spend the rest of my life showing you."

"I was wrong, too, Rand. I was inflexible and ran away instead of trying to understand your feelings. The last twelve months have been hell. More than anything in the world I want to be a good wife to you, make a home for you. We'll work out a compromise we can both live with."

"Annabelle—"

Their mouths fused in passion.

Only a sound rapping on the door could have torn them apart.

"Hey, you two!" Janet's voice resounded. "Everyone out on the terrace is getting a little antsy wondering if there's really going to be a wedding today, especially the minister. What do I tell them?"

Rand lifted his head. "Tell them we'll be there just as soon as Annabelle slips into her wedding dress."

"But it's not here!"

"Yes, it is. Janet sneaked into your closet while you were working on this house and had it pressed for our wedding."

"I love you," she moaned against his lips.

"You don't know the half of it, sweetheart. I told you we make a great team." He crushed her against his heart. "I've waited a lifetime for you, Annabelle. Now that I've found you, I'm not wasting another moment of it."

Joy irradiated her face. "That's how I felt last night

when you became ill. I didn't want to leave you. You might as well know right now that I lied to you. I didn't go to the ballet. I couldn't.''

He already knew that, but her words thrilled him all the same. ''Since confessions are in order, I'll admit that I pretended to be sick so you'd let me stay the night. In fact, I knew you hadn't gone anywhere because your Jeep stayed in the driveway all night.''

''You knew?''

''That's right. You gave me a real scare when you refused to come to Phoenix or open the vacation packet. So I had to come up with a foolproof plan.''

''I always said you were a genius.''

He smiled into her curls. ''I read the fax you sent Janet before I went back to Phoenix. Those words were my lifeline and I clung to them.

''Last night when you allowed me to stay in your father's room and let me use his shaver, I knew you were in love with me. That was all I needed to know to carry out the rest of my plans.''

''Honestly, Rand, when you told me you were getting married… You put me through torture.'' Her voice shook.

''Sweetheart—you invented the word. I just wanted you to be sure of your feelings. Now you're going to have to pay the price of loving me for the rest of your life.''

''Yes, *Ray,* darling,'' she said with feigned meekness.

Rand burst into laughter before he rolled off the bed and helped her to her feet, impatient to embrace a loving future filled with her delightful brand of humor.

Life didn't get better than this, his heart whispered when fifteen minutes later he heard the minister pronounce them man and wife and discovered Annabelle's mouth lifting feverishly to meet his.

"Whenever your husband lets you up for air, may I be the first to kiss the blushing bride?"

Permeating her euphoric daze, Annabelle heard Gerard's voice, then felt him cup her hot face in his hands as her husband let her go with obvious reluctance.

"I've dreamed about doing this for a long time, Mrs. Dunbarton," Gerard whispered before bestowing a tender kiss on her lips. "You just never let me get close enough until now."

"One of these days I'll be kissing you at your own wedding," she whispered back, so full of joy she was floating.

"All right, you two. Break it up. It's my turn," Phil horned in. He was second in the long line of PI's from the agency anxious to congratulate them.

After Cal and Diana took their turn, Roman pulled her into his arms and gave her a long, hard hug. "I guess by now you've figured out I aided and abetted your husband. It was for your own good, Annabelle. You know that now, don't you."

She could only nod.

"You do great work together. Shall I tell him he can come on board permanently? It's up to you."

"I never want him out of my sight. Is that answer enough for you?"

Roman chuckled before kissing her cheek. "Enjoy

your honeymoon, then hurry back. There'll be some challenging new cases. You and Rand can have your pick.''

''I'm so happy,'' she cried, clinging to his shoulder.

''I know,'' he murmured, reading her mind. ''The same thing happened to Brittany and me. You feel like you've died and gone to heaven.''

''Amen,'' Rand interjected huskily, pulling Annabelle back in his arms where she'd always belonged.

Dear Janet—

Greetings from Minorca! I have to tell you this paradise beats Florida hands down. Haven't done any reading. It seems I now have the lifetime job of keeping the big you-know-what happy. So far it hasn't been a problem.

Did I ever tell you this is the job I always wanted? Am reopening the P file.

Love,
A.

P.S. When we get back, I've got plans to help you on *your* P file. I want you to experience this same kind of joy. Every woman should have the privilege of being as happy as Rand makes me.

Love again,
A.

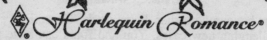

Harlequin Romance

Rebecca Winters writes wonderful romances that pack an emotional punch you'll never forget. Brimful of brides, babies and bachelors, her new trilogy is no exception.

Meet Annabelle, Gerard and Diana. Annabelle and Gerard are private investigators, Diana, their hardworking assistant. Each of them is about to face a rather different assignment—falling in love!

LOVE
undercover

Their mission was marriage!

Books in this series are:

March 1999 #3545
UNDERCOVER FIANCÉE

April 1999 #3549
UNDERCOVER BACHELOR

MAY 1999 #3553
UNDERCOVER BABY

Available wherever Harlequin books are sold.

HARLEQUIN®

Makes any time special ™

Look for a new and exciting series from Harlequin!

HARLEQUIN
Duets™

Two <u>new</u> full-length novels in one book, from some of your favorite authors!

Starting in May, each month we'll be bringing you two new books, each book containing two brand-new stories about the lighter side of love! Double the pleasure, double the romance, for less than the cost of two regular romance titles!

Look for these two new Harlequin Duets™ titles in May 1999:

Book 1:
WITH A STETSON AND A SMILE
by Vicki Lewis Thompson
THE BRIDESMAID'S BET
by Christie Ridgway

Book 2:
KIDNAPPED? by Jacqueline Diamond
I GOT YOU, BABE by Bonnie Tucker

**2 GREAT
STORIES BY
2 GREAT
AUTHORS
FOR 1 LOW
PRICE!**

Don't miss it! Available May 1999 at your favorite retail outlet.

HARLEQUIN®
Makes any time special.™